Thin Air

THIN AIR

ROBERT B. PARKER

G. P. PUTNAM'S SONS   NEW YORK

G. P. PUTNAM'S SONS
Publishers Since 1838
200 Madison Avenue
New York, NY 10016

ISBN 0-399-14020-4

Book design by Julie Duquet

Printed in the United States of America

For Joan: still the taste of wine

Thin Air

He had brought several silk scarves with him in a shopping bag and had used them to gag her and to bind her hands and feet.

"The silk is gentle," he had said to her. "It will not cut you as rope would."

Now she lay helpless, full of fear and anger at her helplessness, on a mattress in the back of an old yellow Ford van, and he drove. As he drove he played with the radio until he found a country-western station.

"Here it is, Angel—90 FM, Rock Country, remember?"

If she raised her head, Lisa could see through the front windshield. The tops of trees went by, and poles and power lines. No buildings. So she wasn't in the city now.

"God, how long's it been, Lees? Ten months and six days. Nearly a year. Man, it's been a hard year . . . but now it's over. We're together."

The van hit a pothole and Lisa bounced uncomfortably on the mattress on the floor of the van. The gag in her mouth was soaked with her saliva; she knew she was drooling a little.

"And that's all that matters," he said. "Whatever happened, happened, and it's over. Now it's all ahead of us. Now we're together."

The van had slowed. They were in traffic. She could hear it, and the van braked often, making her slide around on the mattress. It seemed like a brand-new mattress. Had he bought it for this? Like he'd bought the silk scarves? The van halted altogether. Through the windshield she could see the cab of a trailer truck beside them. If she could only wriggle forward a little maybe the truck driver would see her. But she couldn't. He had looped a rope through her bound ankles and tied it to a ring in the van floor. She was anchored where she was. Traffic started again. The radio played, he sang along with it. The traffic stopped. He turned while they were standing and aimed an ancient video camera at her over the seat.

"Got to get this on tape, our first time together again."

She heard the camera whir.

"Look up, Angel, at the camera."

She buried her face in the mattress. The camera whirred for another moment. Then it stopped and the van started up again.

Chapter 1

I was hitting the heavy bag in Henry Cimoli's Harbor Health Club. The fact that there was a heavy bag to hit was largely out of loyalty to me, and to Hawk, and to Henry past. He has owned the place since it was an ugly gym where fighters trained, having once been a ranked lightweight until Willie Pep urged him into the health club business by knocking him out in the first round of both their fights. It was a lesson in the difference between good and great. Joe Walcott had once taught me the same lesson when I was very young, though it took me longer to learn it.

Outside the boxing cubicle which Henry had squeezed in next to his office was a Babylon of glass and chrome and spandex, where personal trainers, mostly young women with big hair, wearing shiny leotards, trained people on the politically correct way to tone up and be better. Many of them viewed me with suspicion. Henry said it was because I looked like I was there to repossess the equipment.

Henry shmoozed among them with a white silk tee shirt stretched over his body, looking like Arnold Schwarzenegger writ small. He had no shame. When I complained to him that he'd turned the club into a dating bar for the overemployed, he just smiled and rubbed his thumb across his first two fingers. Only if business was slow and he thought no one was watching would he come into the little boxing room and make the speed bag dance. On the other side of Henry's office was a hair salon and a place that gave facials. Upstairs they did aerobics.

I was mainly doing combinations on the heavy bag to keep my hands, wrists, and forearms in shape. I still had to hit people now and again, and I didn't want to hurt myself in the process. I was doing left jab, left jab, right cross, duck, when Frank Belson came in. He had the build for the place, narrow and hard with a thin face. But the tweed scally cap wasn't right, and the tan windbreaker wasn't right, and the permanent blue shadow of a beard that no razor could eliminate wasn't right. No matter what they do, cops finally end up looking like cops. Or crooks, which is why they do well under cover.

"I need to talk," Belson said.

I stopped, breathing hard, my shirt wet with sweat. The opposite end of the room was a full picture window that looked out over Boston harbor. The water was choppy today and scattered with whitecaps. The big airport shuttle from Rowe's Wharf moved serenely across the inconsequential chop. There was nothing else moving in the harbor except the gulls.

"Sure," I said.

"Somewhere else," Belson said.

"Private?"

"Private."

Henry was talking to a plump woman with frizzy blond hair who was trying to do half pushups with the motivational support of her trainer, a sleek young woman with purple tights and a big purple bow, who kept saying things like "excellent" and "you can do it."

"Liz, I've already done eight," the blonde woman said.

"Six," Liz said. "But whatever's comfortable."

I gestured at Henry. He saw me and nodded.

"You're doing terrific, Buffy," Henry said to the blonde. "And it's really beginning to show."

The blonde woman smiled at him as she rested from her six or eight half pushups. Henry turned and walked toward me.

"You're doing great, too," he said.

"Yeah, it'll show soon. You know Frank Belson."

Henry nodded.

"We've met."

Belson said, "Henry."

"Can we use your office for a while?" I said. "Frank and I need to talk."

"Go ahead," Henry said. "I got at least another hour of kissing ass and telling lies before lunch."

"That's called doing business, Henry," I said.

"Yeah. Sure." He looked at me solemnly. "And have a great work out," he said.

Belson and I went into his office and closed the door. I sat in Henry's chair behind his desk. Belson stood, looking out through the glass door at the flashy exercise room. I waited. I'd known Belson for more than twenty years, since the days when I was a cop. He had in that time never asked to speak with me alone, and on any other occasion I could think of would have taken the seat behind the desk. He turned back from staring at the exercise room and looked at the wall behind me. I knew, without looking, because I'd been there often, that there were four or five pictures of Henry when he boxed and at least two pictures of Henry in his current incarnation smiling with celebrated Bostonians who worked out at his club. Belson studied the pictures for a while.

"Henry a good fighter?" he said.

"Yeah."

Belson looked at the wall some more as if memorizing every picture was something he had to do. He put his hands in his hip pockets as he studied the pictures. I leaned back a little in Henry's swivel chair. My breathing had regularized. I felt warm and loose from the exercise. I put my feet up on the desk. Belson stared at the pictures.

"My wife's gone," he said.

"Where?"

"I don't know."

"Why?"

"I don't know."

"Has she left you?" I said.

"I don't know. She's gone. Just disappeared. You know?"

Belson kept his gaze riveted on Henry's wall.

"Tell me about it," I said.

"You know my wife?"

"Yeah, sure. Susan and I were at the wedding."

"Her name's Lisa."

I nodded.

"Second wife, you know."

"Yeah. I know that, Frank."

"And she's a lot younger, and too good looking for me, anyway."

"You think she left you," I said.

"She wouldn't do that. She wouldn't go off without a word."

"You think something happened to her?"

"I checked every hospital in New England," Belson said. "I got a missing person report on the wire all over the Northeast. I called every cop I know personally, told them to look out for her. They'll pay attention. She's a cop's wife."

He turned again and stared out at the exercise room again. Henry's office was silent.

"She could take care of herself. She's been around."

"You and she been having trouble?" I said.

His back still to me, he shook his head.

"You want me to look for her?"

He was motionless. I waited. Finally he spoke.

"No. I can do that. We don't find her soon, I'll take time off," he said. "I know how to look."

I nodded.

"What's her maiden name?" I said.

"St. Claire."

"She got family somewhere?"

Belson turned and looked straight at me for the first time.

"I don't want to talk about it," he said.

I nodded. Belson stared out at the people exercising in their variegated spandex. Sometimes I thought it was like golf; people did it so they could wear the clothes. But then I noticed that most people looked funny in the clothes and decided I was wrong. Or most of them knew themselves but slightly. The silence in Henry's office was stifling. I waited. Belson stared.

Finally, I said, "You don't want to talk about it, Frank, and you don't want me to help you look, how come you came here and told me about it?"

He stared silently for another time, then he spoke without turning.

"Happened to you," he said. "Ten, twelve years ago."

"Susan left for a while," I said.

"She told you she was going."

"She left a note," I said.

Belson stared silently through the window. The exercisers were exercising, and the trainers were training, but I knew Belson wasn't looking at them. He wasn't looking at anything.

"She came back," he said.

"So to speak," I said. "We worked it out."

"Lisa didn't leave no note," Belson said.

Anything I could think of to say about that was not encouraging.

"When I find her I'll ask her about that," he said.

He turned finally and looked straight at me.

"Thanks for your time," he said and went out the office door.

It was dark when the van stopped. She could hear a radio playing somewhere and a dog barking. He got out of the car and came around and opened the van doors. She wriggled into a sitting position. The camera light was bright in her eyes. The camera whirred.

"Look at me, honey," he said. "We are home now . . . No, look this way . . . turn your head . . . come on, do not be such a tease."

Behind him a short man appeared pushing a hand truck with a tarpaulin over his shoulder. The camera continued to whir.

"Just give me a minute . . . I want to get everything . . . you don't get it and then later you are sorry . . . wait until we have children, I'll be behind this camera all the time."

The whirring stopped. "Okay, Rico," he said, "take her up."

With a buck knife, Rico cut the rope that anchored her to the floor of the van. He picked up her purse from the floor of the van and hung it over one handle of the hand truck. Then he pushed her flat and rolled her into the tarp. He heaved her onto the hand truck, strapped her to it, and wheeled her away. She could see nothing. The tarpaulin smelled of turpentine and mildew. She heard a door open and felt the hand truck begin to bump up some stairs. She jostled on it like a sack of potatoes. It was what she felt like, a helpless, inert, jostling sack of Lisa. The frame of the hand truck hurt her as it dug into her side. She couldn't complain. She couldn't speak. It was too much. She couldn't bear it. She could feel her breath slipping in and out, feel the sweat soaking her clothing, feel the saliva-soaked gag in her mouth. The hand truck bumped and then slid along smoothly and then began to bump again. She twisted futilely inside her canvas and tried to scream and couldn't.

Chapter 2

That night Susan and I were having an early supper at the East Coast Grill, where our waitress was an attractive blonde woman who sculpted during the daytime, and supported her habit by waiting tables. The cuisine at East Coast is barbecue, and no one who went there, except Susan, was able to eat wisely or drink in moderation. I made no attempt at either. I ordered spare ribs, beans, coleslaw, a side of watermelon, and extra corn bread, and drank some Rolling Rock beer while they cooked the ribs over the open wood-fired barbecue pit in the back. Susan had a margarita, no salt, while she waited for her tuna steak cooked rare, and a green salad. When the tuna came, she cut two thirds of it off, and put it aside on her bread plate.

"Susan," I said. "You have worked heavy labor all day. You are already in better shape than Dame Margot Fonteyn."

"I should be. Margot Fonteyn is dead," Susan said. "We'll bring that home for Pearl. She likes fresh tuna."

"Why not throw caution to the wind?" I said. "Have salt with your margarita. Eat all of the tuna."

"I threw caution to the wind when I took up with you," she said.

"And wisely so," I said. "But why not give yourself a little leeway when you eat?"

"Shut up."

"Ah ha," I said. "I hadn't considered that aspect of it."

I picked up a spare rib and worked on it carefully for a time. I had never succeeded in keeping the sauce off my shirt front in the years I'd been coming here. On the other hand, I had never spilled any on my gun.

"How's Frank?" Susan said.

I shrugged. "He doesn't say much. But it's eating him up. He could barely talk when I saw him."

"No word on Lisa?"

"No."

"You think she left him?"

"He says she wouldn't go without telling him, but . . ."

"But people do things under stress that you'd never expect," Susan said.

I nodded. I worked on my ribs for a bit. The room smelled of wood smoke. The beer was cold. There was a bottle of hot sauce on the table. Susan poured some on her tuna.

"Good God," I said. "Are you suicidal?"

She ate some.

"Hot," she said.

"They use that stuff to force confessions," I said.

"I like it."

I ate some corn bread and drank some beer. The restaurant had been built in what was probably once a variety store. Outside the plate-glass windows in front, the early spring evening was settling over Inman Square. Car lights were just beginning to impact on the darkening ether around them.

"I've seen Frank walk into a dark building where people were shooting. And you'd have thought he was going in to buy a Table Talk Junior Pie."

"How'd it hit you when I left?"

"Hard to remember. It was awhile, you know?"

"Un huh. What was I wearing when you first met me?"

"Black silk blouse with big sleeves, white slacks. Blouse open at the neck. Silver chain around the neck. Silver bracelet. Small, coiled silver earrings. I think you had a hint of blue eye shadow. And your hair was in sort of a page boy."

"Un huh."

We were quiet for a moment. I broke off another piece of corn bread and ate it.

"Okay, Miss Shrink. I remember every detail of when we met, and not much of anything about when we split."

"Un huh."

"Surely this is fraught with meaning. And if you say 'un huh' one more time I won't let you watch when I shower."

"Heavens," Susan said.

"So what are you getting at?"

"Men like Frank Belson, like Quirk, like you, are what they are in part because they are contained. They can control their feelings, they can control themselves, because they let nothing in. They don't talk a great deal. They don't show a great deal."

"Except to the woman," I said.

"Have you ever noticed," Susan said, "how little affection you have for small talk in general, and how freely you talk with me?"

"At times it approaches prattle," I said.

"I think it is superior to prattle. But aside from me, to whom are you closest?"

"Paul Giacomin and Hawk."

"There's a parley. Do you and Paul prattle?"

"No."

"Do you prattle with Hawk?"

"Christ no," I said.

"Or Belson, or Quirk, or Henry Cimoli, or your friend the gunfighter?"

"Vinnie Morris?"

"Yes, Vinnie. Do they prattle?"

"Probably to the woman," I said. "Except Hawk. I don't think Hawk ever prattles."

"About Hawk, I remain agnostic," Susan said. "Being male is a complicated thing. Being a black male is infinitely more complicated."

The blonde waitress came by and gave me another bottle of Rolling Rock without being asked. I knew she was taken, and so was I. But adoption might still be possible.

"Think about yourself," Susan said. "You're like a goddamned armadillo. You give very little, you ask very little, and the only way to hurt you is to get inside the armor."

"Which is what happened to Frank," I said.

"Lisa got inside," Susan said. "And he gave her everything he gave to no one else. He gave her all of himself. All of the self no one else sees, or hears of, or even knows exists. Which is probably quite a heavy load for her, or any woman, to have dumped on her."

"You seem able to handle it," I said.

"Able and eager," Susan said. "But in Frank's case, when Lisa found what he had given her, which is to say his whole self, insufficient, or he feared she found it insufficient, there was no armor to protect him. . . ."

"The first marriage probably wore him down some," I said.

Susan smiled at me.

"It would," she said. "I gather his first marriage failed almost at once, and kept failing for twenty-something years. That would rob him of the thing that keeps you, not pain-free certainly, but"—Susan searched for a phrase—"on course," she said finally and shrugged at the inadequacy of the phrase.

I didn't think it was inadequate. I thought it was a dandy phrase.

"What's that?" I said.

She thought about it for a moment, the tip of her tongue showing on her sucked-in lower lip, as it always did when she is considering something.

"Self-regard, I suppose, is as good a word as any," Susan said. "At bottom you are pleased with yourself."

"Self-regard? How about saying I have an optimally integrated self? Wouldn't that sound better?"

"Of course it would. I wish I'd said it."

"Go ahead, claim you did," I said. "In a while I'll think so too."

"It's what made you survive our separation, the thing you got before you knew it, from your father and your uncles."

Dinner was over, the last Rolling Rock had been drunk. Susan had guzzled nearly a third of her glass of red wine.

"Heaviest rap I've had in a long time," I said.

"Were you able to follow the hard parts okay?"

"I think so," I said. "But the effort has exacerbated my libido."

"Is there any effort that does not exacerbate your libido?" Susan said.

"I don't think so," I said. "Shall we go back to your place and explore my vulnerability?"

"What about Pearl?"

"She's a dog. Let her explore her own vulnerability," I said.

"I'll ask her to go in the living room," Susan said. "Was I really wearing blue eye shadow when you met me?"

"Un huh."

"God, never tell the fashion police."

The first thing she was aware of as she came to consciousness was a silent voice.

"Frank will find me," the voice said. "Frank will find me."

Then she smelled the roach powder. She had once lived in an apartment where the janitor put it out every day to fight the roaches. She knew the smell; it seemed almost reassuring in its familiarity. She opened her eyes. She was in bed, with a purple silk coverlet over her, her head propped on several ivory lace pillows. She tried to sit up. She was still tied. The knotted scarf was still in her mouth. She could hear someone laughing. It sounded familiar. Silly laughter, happy and slightly manic. Around the room were television monitors, some on light stands, some suspended from the high ceiling, at least five of them. On each monitor Lisa saw herself, her head thrown back, laughing. She had on a daring swim suit, and in the background the ocean advanced and receded. She remembered the day. They had been at Crane's Beach. She had brought chicken and French bread and nectarines and wine.

She heard herself shriek with laughter as he poured a little wine down her bra. The sound went suddenly silent, leaving only the noiseless images of her giggling on the silent screens. Suddenly, shocking the darkness in the room where she lay helplessly watching herself, there was the sudden white light of the video camera. She heard the whir of the tape moving, and the whine of the zoom lens. He came out of the darkness behind the monitors, with his camera.

"Don't you love Crane's Beach, Angel?" he said, the camera in front of his face. "We'll go there again... Look at us, is that great?... Me Tarzan, you Jane."

On the monitors, there was a shot of her home in Jamaica Plain, then a splice jump and her face appeared on the screen, close up, her mouth contorted into something almost like a grin by the tightness of the gag. The camera zoomed back. She was on the floor in the back of the van, her eyes shiny in the pitiless light. On the bed she turned her head away. He reached out and gently turned it back.

"I have to see you, baby, don't be coy."

And he filmed her in time present watching films he'd taken of her in times past.

Chapter 3

I sat inside the frosted glass cubicle where the Homicide Commander had his office and talked with Martin Quirk about Belson.

"Frank's taking some time off," Quirk said.

His blue blazer hung on a hanger on a hook inside his door. He wore a white shirt and a maroon knit tie and his thick hands rested quietly on the near-empty desk between us. He was always quiet, except when he got mad, then he was quieter. Nobody much wanted to make him mad.

"I know," I said. "You know why?"

"Needed a rest."

"You know about his wife?"

"Yes."

"Me too," I said.

"What do you know?"

"I know she's gone."

Quirk nodded.

"Okay," he said. "So I don't have to be cute."

"Is that what you were being?"

"Yeah."

"He's afraid she left him," I said.

"Happens," Quirk said.

"You've never had the experience," I said.

"You have."

"Yeah."

"I remember."

"There's nothing logical about your first reactions," I said.

"Must be why they call it crazy time."

"That's why," I said. "What do you know about her?"

"No, you got it wrong," Quirk said. "I'm the copper. I say stuff like that to you."

"Frank won't talk about her."

Quirk nodded. "But you, being a fucking Eagle Scout, are nosing around."

"That's how I like to think of it," I said.

"Frank's kind of fucked up about this."

"So what do you know about her?"

"Her name's Lisa St. Claire. She's a disc jockey at a station in Proctor, which is one of those jerkwater cities up by New Hampshire."

"I know Proctor," I said.

"Good for you," Quirk said. "Frank met her about a year ago. In the bar at the Charles Hotel. Frank had just gone through the divorce. The old lady didn't let go easy. You ever meet adorable Kitty?"

I nodded.

"So Lisa looked good to him. Hell, she looks good to me, and I'm happily married. Frank probably did the I'm-a-police-detective trick, always works great."

"How the hell do you know?" I said.

"Used to work great for me."

"You got married before you were a detective."

Quirk grinned.

"I used to lie," he said. "Anyway, she and Frank started going out. They moved in together about a month later, his old lady had the house. Maybe six months ago they got married and bought that place out near the pond."

"She got money?"

Quirk shrugged.

"How much does a disc jockey make?"

"More than a cop."

"'Cause they're more valuable," he said. "Frank worked a lot of overtime, probably had a little something put away, himself."

"That his wife didn't get?"

"He saw that coming for a long time," Quirk said. "Might have had a few bearer bonds someplace."

"You know how old Lisa is?"

"Nope, I'd guess around thirty. What do you think?"

"Lot younger than Frank," I said.

"And better looking. Frank was fucking blown away by how good looking she was."

"Yeah," I said, "but is she a nice person?"

"Maybe we'll find that out," Quirk said.

"You know where she's from?"

Quirk shrugged.

"Family?"

Shrug.

"You know where she worked before Proctor?"

"No."

"Ever hear her program?"

"No. I'm too busy listening to my Prince albums."

"He doesn't call himself Prince anymore."

"Who gives a fuck," Quirk said.

"Nobody I know," I said. "She been married before?"

"I don't know."

"Thirty's kind of old for a first marriage," I said.

"For crissake, Spenser, you've never been married at all."

"Sure, that's odd, too. But I'm not missing."

"Kids get laid now. They live with people. They don't marry as early."

"How old were you?" I said.

"Twenty," Quirk said.

"Better to marry than burn," I said.

"Worked out okay for me," Quirk said. "But a lot of people got married so they could fuck six times a week. Then in a while they only felt like fucking once a week and had to talk to each other in between. Created a lot of drunks."

"You think she left him?" I said.

"I don't know," Quirk said. "If she left him it'll kill him. If she didn't leave him . . . where the fuck is she?"

"Hard to know what to root for," I said.

The window behind Quirk looked out into Stanhope Street, which was little more than an alley. If you stood up and looked, you could see Bertucci's Pizza, where the Red Coach Grill once was. A pigeon settled on Quirk's window ledge and sidled across it, puffing up his feathers as he went. He turned sideways and looked in at us with one eye. Behind me in the squad room the phone rang periodically, sometimes only once, sometimes for much too long. A phone call to Homicide didn't usually bring good news.

I stood up. The pigeon watched me.

"I hear anything, I'll let you know," Quirk said.

I opened Quirk's door. As I went out, the pigeon flew away.

*S*he was out of bondage. And she was alone. On the monitors were images of him, carefully untying the scarves. The release helped reduce her panic a little. She could at least move. She could speak, though there was no one but him to speak to.

"We will save these scarves, amor mio," he said on the monitors. "They are part of our reuniting."

She sat on the edge of her bed waiting for the pins and needles of reawakened circulation to subside. It was a huge, four-poster Victorian bed fitted with pale lavender satin sheets covered with a thick damask canopy. Around the bed were theater flats, creating a tarnished and shabby illusion of green meadows, and willow trees, archaic stone walls, and an elongated English pointer in field pose. In the distance, lambs grazed under the gaze of a young shepherd with no shoes and a crook. A winding road dwindled in geometric perspective through the meadow, and curved out of sight behind the wall. Some of the flats she knew were from a Children's Theater production of Rumpelstiltskin. How he had gotten them she didn't know. Behind the flats the windows were boarded up, and the light came from a series of clamp lights on the web of pipes near the black painted ceiling, as well as the glow of the television monitors, which looped the same sequences over and over. The monitors were silent again. He seemed to control the sound whimsically. There were gauze cloths draped among the lights, masking the ceiling and creating a tattered semblance of gossamer eternity above. A big oak wardrobe stood against the wall opposite the foot of the bed. Its double doors were open, and the wardrobe was packed with theatrical costumes. In the far wall to the right of the bed was a doorway. She got up when she could and went to it, walking with difficulty, her legs still numb and tingling. The door was locked. She hadn't thought it would be open. She turned and began to circle the room, running her hands around the black plywood panels that had been nailed in place over the windows. One of the panels was hinged on one side and padlocked on the other. Another had an air conditioner cut into it. All of them were impenetrable. She opened her mouth and worked her jaw a little. Her mouth, which had felt so wet when she was gagged, now felt dry and stiff. She said "Hello" out loud a couple of times to see if she could speak. The noise was rusty and small in the sealed room. She felt the claustrophobic panic again. She was untied, but she was not free. To the left of the armoire was a bathroom, the door ajar, the light on dimly. The walls were pink plastic tile. There was a pink chenille cover on the toilet seat, and the one-piece fiberglass shower stall had a pink tinted glass door on it. There were flowers in a vase, and a thick pink rug on the floor. There was no window. Behind her she heard the camera sound.

"You should shower, querida. There is French milled soap, and lilac shampoo, and there are fresh clothes for you in the armoire. . . . Do not be shy . . . I will have everything on tape . . . we will watch it all together when we are old."

She stared at him, unmoving. She was wearing the sweat-soaked blouse and jeans that she'd been wearing when he took her.

"Take off your clothes, chiquita, you need to shower and change."

She continued to stare at him. She had been naked with him before. They had made love often. But now it was as if a stranger had ordered her to disrobe in public. She could think of no words.

"Do it," he said and his voice was full of hate, "or I will have it done."

She stared at him still, and the camera continued to whir. She felt the bottomlessness of herself, the sense of weakness that raced along her arms and clenched in her stomach. It was an old feeling. She'd had it many times. She didn't want to. She couldn't bear to. She was being forced to. There was no way not to. The two of them stood poised like that, in a kind of furious immobility for an infinite time in which all there was was the sound of the camera tape rolling, and of her breath and his, both slightly raspy. Helpless, she thought. I'm helpless again. Then, slowly, she began to unbutton her blouse.

Chapter 4

I sat in a coffee shop on Columbus Avenue with Frank Belson and drank a cup of decaffeinated coffee on an ugly spring day with the sky a hard gray and a spit of rain mixed with snow flakes in the air. He hadn't found his wife yet.

"You meet her before you got divorced from Kitty?" I said, mostly to be saying something.

"No."

"So she wasn't the reason for the divorce," I said.

"The divorce was just making it official," he said. "The marriage had been fucked for a long time."

I was on one of my periodic attempts to give up coffee. The previous failures were discouraging, but not final. I stirred more sugar into my decaf to disguise it.

"Kitty was bad," Belson said, looking at the faintly iridescent surface of his real coffee. "Hysterical, nervous—thought fucking was only a way to get children. Didn't want children, but didn't want anyone to get ahead of her by having them first. You know?"

"I was never one of Kitty's rooters," I said.

"Money," he said. "I never saw anyone worry about money like her. How to get it, how to save it, why we shouldn't spend it, why I should earn more. How we were going to hold up our head in the neighborhood when

Trudy Fitzgerald's husband made twice what I did being an engineer at Sylvania. If I would of paid her to fuck she'd have done it every night."

"What could be more natural," I said.

"'Course, after the first couple months I would probably have paid her not to. But we had the kid and then we had a couple more. Kitty always knew the correct number of children to have. She had all the damn rules down, you know? Whether you needed a house on the water, whether the girls should go to parochial school, whether you should add salt to the water before you boiled it, what kind of underwear a decent woman wore."

He stopped talking for a while. He still held the coffee, but he didn't drink it. I waited. A couple of cops came in and sat at the counter. Belson nodded at them without speaking. Both cops ordered coffee, one had a piece of pineapple pie with it.

"But you didn't get a divorce," I said.

"We were Catholics since twenty fucking thousand years ago. And we had the kids, and, shit, the time went by and we'd been married twenty-three years and barely spoke. I worked a lot of overtime."

"And then you met Lisa," I said.

"Yeah. Cambridge had picked up a guy named Wozak on an assault warrant, thought he might be a guy we were looking for, clipped an informant we use, junkie named Eddie Navarrone. Eddie's no loss, but it's a departmental policy to discourage murder when we can, so I went over and talked with Wozak. Might be our guy, I'm not sure. Cambridge has got him cold, so he's not going anywhere. At least until some judge walks him because he was denied health insurance."

"Or they got no place to put him," I said.

Belson shrugged, his back still to me, staring out at the grim spring day.

"Oughta put him in the ground," Belson said.

I ordered another decaf. Belson's coffee must have turned cold in his cup while we talked. He still held it, and he didn't drink it. He glanced out at the early spring snow spatter.

"You seen any robins yet?" Belson said.

"No."

"Me either."

"Did you meet Lisa in Cambridge?" I said.

"Yeah."

"You want to tell me about it or shall I make something up and you tell me if I'm getting warm?"

Belson took a sip of coffee, shook his head and put it down.

"It's about five-thirty. I'm at the bar at the Charles Hotel, having a vodka and tonic. And she's at the bar. It's not a big bar, you ever been there?"

"Yeah."

"She had on a yellow dress, and one of those hats with the brim turned up all around that women wear right down over their eyes, and she's drinking the same thing. And she says to me, 'What kind of vodka?' And I say, 'Stoli,' and she smiles at me, says, 'That's what I used to drink. Great minds, huh?' "

The two cops at the counter finished their coffee, got up, and headed for the door. Belson watched them go.

"Area B guys," he said absently.

"So it began," I said.

"Yeah. And she asked me what I did and I told her and she said, 'Are you carrying a gun?' and I said, 'Yeah, pointing your finger at them doesn't work,' and she laughed and we talked the rest of the night. And I didn't go home with her, but I got her number and I called her the next day."

He paused again, watching the two cops get into a gray Ford sedan and pull away from the hydrant they'd parked on. Then he spoke again, still staring after the departing car.

"She wasn't, isn't, like anyone else. She was all there in the right-now, you know? She was everything she was, all the time. Nothing held back, no games. And the first time we went to bed she said to me, 'I'll tell you anything about myself you want to know, but if it's up to me, I'd like to pretend life started the night we met.' And I said, 'Sure. No past. No nothing, just you and me.' And that's how it's been. I don't know anything about her except with me."

I waited, sipping my decaf. Belson sat quietly.

"You think Kitty might have anything to do with Lisa going away?"

"No," Belson said slowly. "I've thought about it. And no. Kitty's a bad asshole, but she's not that kind of bad asshole. She's in Florida with her sister, been there since February tenth."

She could have had it done, I thought. But that implied things it would do Belson no good to think about.

"You think you might want to look into Lisa's background a little, now that this has happened?"

"Yeah," Belson said. "I haven't, but I know I have to."

After a while I said, "You'll find her."

"Yeah," he said softly. "I will."

t was a good shower. Lots of hot water. Lots of water pressure. The water washed over her, soaking her hair, sluicing over her body. She scrubbed herself vigorously, lathering her body, shampooing her hair, washing away the grime and sweat of her captivity and, as much as she could, the fear. He was there with his camera, open-shuttered and passive. Could she keep something? Keep some piece of Lisa intact? Nearly im- mobilized with terror, feeling the hopeless weight of it dragging at her every movement, could there be some part of her that could remain Lisa? She stood fully erect and made no attempt to conceal her nakedness. She couldn't keep him from seeing her. But she could get clean, and goddamn him, she wasn't going to cower. But she was so frightened, so alone, that she knew how thin her resolve was. It would not take much more than this to make her cower. She amended her resolve. I will try not to cower, she thought. When she was through she stepped from the shower and toweled herself dry, making no attempt to hide herself, looking straight at him and his implacable lens. Frank will find me, she thought. She hung the towel on its hook beside the shower and walked straight at the camera lens. He backed away from her as she walked, into the bedroom. Her clothes were gone, and laid out on the bed was fresh lingerie and a costume, a black flapper dress, with beads along the hemline.

"You want me to wear this?" Lisa said.

It was the first sound she had made other than the hellos. Her voice star- tled her. It sounded ordinary. It sounded like the voice of someone who had never been carried from her home in bondage and locked up in a dark place somewhere.

"Every day we will be different," he said.

"Sure," Lisa said.

She began to dress. Frank will find me. The phrase was like a mantra. She said it to herself the way someone might mumble a prayer. She slid the dress over her head. It fit. It would. He would know her size. What would Frank tell her to do? What should she do? Frank would tell her to be ready. Frank would tell her not to wait for him. Frank would tell her to get herself out. I'll try, she thought. I can try. When she was dressed, he seated her at the table. The light from a single candle played on his face and brightened the glassware. The sound of the monitors was shut off. The rest of the room was dark and the darkness came very close about them. He was wearing a starched collar and his hair was slicked back. He raised his glass to her.

"Welcome home, Angel."

She shook her head. Maybe first I can try reason, she thought. Even silently spoken, her speech sounded shaky inside her head.

"No?" he said.

"No," she said. "My home is with my husband."

"That is over, Angel. It was a mistake. It will be corrected."

He sipped some wine from his glass and poured a little more. He smiled at her gently as if he had settled a question important to a child. She felt a flash of anger.

"It can't be corrected, Luis. I love him."

He frowned momentarily, and then his face smoothed again and he inclined his head indulgently.

"I won't say I didn't love you," Lisa said. "I think I probably did. It was real. But it wasn't permanent."

She felt as if she had to get air in after nearly every word. Her speech seemed halting to her. She was so frightened she was speaking so carefully. He didn't seem to notice. He smiled at her, indulgently, and took a cigar from his pocket. He trimmed it carefully with a small silver knife and lit it carefully, turning the cigar so that it burned evenly. Then he put the lighter away and puffed placidly on the cigar. On the soundless monitors her image, bound on the floor of his van, moved on the screens, lit by the harsh light bar of his camera. She looked away.

"It couldn't be permanent," she said. The words were getting away from her. She could feel them start to bubble carelessly out, before they'd been thought about, before they'd been sanitized. "Because you never saw me when you looked at me. You saw a fucking bowling trophy. Some sex, some fun, to lock up in the trophy case when not in use. Like now, like I am in your goddamned camera."

He inhaled slowly and let the smoke drift back out. He smiled at her dreamily, leaning back in his chair, turning his wine glass slowly by the stem.

"Angel, I have loved you since I met you. It is I who am locked up—in your eyes, in your lips, by your body."

"That's exactly the flowery bullshit that you used to smother me with. And the more I tried to be an actual goddamned human being, the more flowery bullshit you shoveled. It has never been about me. It is always about you and how I make you feel."

The skin around his eyes looked stiff, as if someone had pulled it too tight. *She seemed unable to stop the words as they tumbled out, she was frightened to be saying them, but she couldn't stop. If she could just pause, get a breath, get control.*

"Frank takes me seriously," she said.

"And I . . ." he said, appalled at what he was hearing. *"I do . . . not . . . take you seriously. I . . . who nearly died when you left me. Who spent every moment since you left looking for you? I who am nothing without you. I do not take you seriously?"*

She felt the shaky feeling spread from the pit of her stomach and dart along her arms and legs and up her spine. And yet, at the center of herself there was starting to be something else, an ill-formed kernel of self that would not yield. That would not, or, the thought skittered briefly past her consciousness, could not, cease to be Lisa. She would fight him, as best she could, with whatever she had. She had come too far, been through too much, before finally becoming Lisa. She would not go back. She would rather die than go back. She stared at him for a moment leaning intensely toward her.

"No," she said. *"You take yourself seriously."*

His face seemed to crumple and then recompose. He puffed on the cigar for a moment and there was something flickering in his eyes that frightened her intensely.

"And so shall you," he said.

Chapter 5

I was in my office. Outside my window it was a bright hard spring day, not very warm, but no wind and a lot of sunshine. There were spring clothes in the shops along Newbury Street, and somebody had put a few tables outside some of the cafes. It was still too brisk for anyone to sit outside, but it was a harbinger, and it made me feel good. Breakfast was over and I was planning lunch when Quirk called.

"Belson got shot last night," he said. "I'll pick you up outside your office in two minutes."

"He alive?" I said.

"Half," Quirk said and hung up.

I was outside wearing my authentic replica A-2 leather jacket with the collar up when an unmarked black Ford with a buggy whip antenna swung into the curb. Quirk was in the back, and a Homicide dick named Malone was driving. I got in the back with Quirk, and Malone pulled away from the curb, hit the siren, ran a red light and headed down Boylston Street.

"Belson was coming home last night, around eight o'clock, and while he was unlocking his front door somebody pumped three nine-millimeter slugs into him from behind," Quirk said. "One broke the left scapula, one punched a hole in his right side and went on through. One is still there, right near his spine, down low."

"He going to make it," I said.

"Probably," Quirk said. "They don't know how soon he'll walk."

"Shooter didn't group his shots very tight," I said.

"We noticed that too," Quirk said. "On the other hand, he apparently hit all three shots he took. We haven't found any other slugs."

"So he's a pretty good shot," I said, "but maybe excited."

"Maybe."

Malone yanked the car down Arlington Street and turned left on St. James.

"He conscious?" I said.

"In and out," Quirk said. "But last time he was in, he said he wanted to see you."

With the siren full on we went through Copley Square, and out Huntington Avenue.

"What hospital?" I said.

"Brigham," Quirk said.

"Any suspects?"

"No."

We went out Huntington, turned down Francis and pulled in under the portico at the main hospital entrance, and parked. A fat black woman in a hospital security uniform came toward us as we got out, waving us away. Malone flashed his badge and she stopped and nodded and walked away.

Belson was in the intensive care unit, a sheet pulled up to the middle of his chest. There was an IV into a vein on the back of his right hand. His left arm was in a cast. Lee Farrell was there, with his hips on a windowsill. There was another Homicide cop I didn't know sitting in a chair by Belson's bedside with a tape recorder. The recorder wasn't picking anything up. Belson appeared to be sleeping. I nodded at Farrell.

The cop with the tape recorder said, "He's coked to the eyeballs, Lieutenant. He hasn't said a word."

Quirk nodded.

"Frank," he said. "Spenser's here."

Belson made no movement for maybe twenty seconds, then his eyes opened. He shifted his eyeballs slowly toward Quirk's voice and slowly past Quirk and looked at me. The cop beside the bed turned on the tape recorder.

"Talk . . . to . . . Spenser," he said slowly in a very soft voice. Everything he did was slow, as if the circuits weren't connected very well.

I moved a little closer to the bed and bent over.

"What do you need?" I said.

His eyes remained fixed for a moment at the spot where I had been, then slowly they moved and, even more slowly, they refocused on me.

"You . . . find . . . her," he said.

"Lisa," I said.

"Can't . . . look . . . now. You . . . look."

"Yeah," I said. "I'll find her."

Belson was silent for a while. His eyes were on me, but they didn't seem to be seeing me. Then he moved his lips carefully. For a moment no sound came.

Then he said, "Good."

Everyone was quiet in the room. Belson kept his blank eyes on me. Then he nodded faintly and let his eyes close and didn't move. The cop with the tape recorder turned it off.

In the corridor, Quirk said, "You chase the wife, we'll chase the shooter. They turn out to be connected, we'll cooperate in our common endeavor."

"He say anything I can use?"

"He hasn't said anything anybody can use. Even if he was lucid, I don't think he knows what hit him. He got it in the back and he never cleared his piece."

"A real pro," I said, "would have made sure it was finished."

"A real amateur wouldn't have hit all three shots," Quirk said. "Maybe something scared him off."

"If something did, be nice to find out what it was and talk to it."

"We're looking," Quirk said.

"Doctors give you any idea how long before he can talk more than he's doing now?"

"No. They've shot him full of hop right now, and they say he'll need it for a while."

"So I'm on my own," I said.

"Aren't you always?" Quirk said.

We walked slowly through the hospital corridors to the elevator.

"You want to look through Frank's house?" Quirk said. He handed me a new key with a little tag hanging from it on a string. On the tag "Belson, FD" was written in blue ink.

"I suppose I got to," I said.

"Don't get delicate," Quirk said. "It's a case now."

Chapter 6

Belson and his bride had a condominium on Perkins Street in Jamaica Plain right next to Brookline. It was a good-looking collection of gray and white Cape Cod-style semihouses attached in angular ways and scattered in a seemingly random pattern like an actual neighborhood that had evolved naturally. Across the street and down a slope behind me was Jamaica Pond, gleaming in the late March afternoon as if it were still a place where Wampanoags gathered. Across the pond, cars went too fast along the Jamaica Way, and in the distance the downtown city rose clean and pleasant-looking against a pale sky in the very early spring.

I could see the gouge where someone had dug out a slug from the door frame, about hip high. I opened the door and went in. I didn't like it much. It made me uncomfortable to nose around in the privacy of somebody I'd known for twenty years. I'd seen Belson at home once or twice with the first wife in an ugly frame house in Roslindale. I'd been in Belson's new living room once, after the wedding. But now I felt like an intruder. On the other hand, I had to start somewhere. I didn't know what Belson had done, looking for his wife. Had he listened to her messages? Checked her mail? Looked for missing clothing? Purse? I had to start from scratch.

I was in a small entryway. A breakfast nook was to my left. The living room was straight ahead. On my right was a stairway to the second floor, and under the stairs was a lavatory. The kitchen was between the breakfast

nook and the living room. Nothing was very big. Everything was very new.
There was a fireplace in one corner of the living room. There was a Sub
Zero refrigerator in the kitchen, and a Jenn Air cook stove, a Kitchen Aid
dishwasher, a trash compactor, a microwave, some terra cotta tile, and a variety of nuts and grains in clear acrylic canisters, which appeared never to
have been opened. It wasn't much different than a lot of condos I'd been in,
where mass production cut the building costs and the builder spent money
on accessories that made the owners feel with it.

Upstairs a huge draped four-poster filled up the bedroom. There was a
Jacuzzi in the bathroom. The third room was small but served at least to acknowledge the possibility of a child or a guest. It had been converted to a
study which obviously belonged to Lisa.

There was a picture of her and Frank framed on the wall. Short blonde
hair, wide mouth, big eyes. She was quite striking, and even more so in person, because she had a good athletic body, and a lot of spring. Being a
trained detective, I had taken note of the body at the wedding. Next to the
picture was a framed award certificate announcing that Lisa St. Claire of
WPOM-FM served with honor as chairman of the media division of the
Proctor United Fund. Below the certificate, on the desk, was a Macintosh
computer, a cordless phone setup, and an answering machine. The digital
display said that there were four messages. I punched the All Messages button.

"Hey, St. Claire, it's your buddy Tiffany. I'll pick you up for class
tonight about seven, give us time for coffee . . . Lisa, it's Dr. Wilson's office, confirming your appointment at two forty-five on Tuesday for clean-
ing . . . Lisa, how lovely to hear your voice. I hope soon to see
you . . . Honey, I get off about seven tonight. I'll pick up some Chinese
food on the way home. I love you."

The phone had a redial button. I punched it. At the other end a voice
said, "Homicide." I hung up. Her last phone call had been to her husband.
Probably wanted extra mu shu chicken and I love you too . . . or maybe just
the mu shu.

Aside from Belson, nobody on the machine meant anything to me. If he
were functional, I could have played the messages and asked him to iden-
tify the callers. But he wasn't. I listened to the messages again and made
notes.

The first message was self-explanatory if I knew what class, and where
and who Tiffany was, which I didn't. Tiffany called Lisa by her maiden
name, if that meant anything. I wondered for a moment if "maiden name"
was any longer acceptable. What would be the correct locution? Prenuptial
name? Birth name? Nonspousal designation?

Unless it was a coded message, the second one was a dentist. The third message was a man who might, I couldn't tell for sure, have an accent. The fourth one was Belson. I looked around the study. There was a catalog from Merrimack State College. That would explain the class. I opened the desk drawer and found three Bic pens, medium black, some candy-striped paper clips, some rubber bands, an instruction manual for the answering machine, a battered wooden ruler, a letter opener, a roll of stamps, and bills from three credit card companies. I put the bills in my coat pocket. There was no phone book; it was probably in her purse. On her desk calendar pad at the top, associated with no specific date, the word *Vaughn* was written in several different decorative ways, as if someone had doodled it while talking on the phone. There wasn't anything else. I went into their bedroom and looked around. There was no sign of her purse. I opened a closet. It was hers. The scent of her cologne was strong. There was no purse in the closet. I opened the other closet. It was Belson's. I closed it. I looked at her bureau and shook my head. I declined to rummage further in the bedroom.

I took a tour of the downstairs, looking in closets and cupboards. There was no sign of a purse. If she hadn't taken her purse, it was a good bet she didn't leave on her own. It didn't mean she had left voluntarily. But it was hopeful. Or not. I wasn't exactly sure what I should be hoping for. If she had simply walked out on him without a word, that would be pretty awful. If someone had forced her to leave, that would be pretty awful. Probably better just to find her, and when I did then I'd know.

I took the calendar with me when I left the condo and walked back to my car. There was still snow in some shadowed areas, and ugly mounds of it compacted by salt and sand and pollution squatted where the plows had tossed it in the winter. But there was also bird song and the ground was spongy, and somewhere doubtless a goat-footed balloon man was whistling far and wee. I drove back to my office with the windows down.

He had her dressed in a Southern Belle costume today, like Scarlett O'Hara. He himself was wearing some sort of riverboat gambler getup with a black string tie and ruffled-front shirt. There was some salad and some French bread and a bottle of champagne on the table. He poured her some wine and handed it to her.

"I don't drink anymore, Luis."

"Not even a little champagne?"

"I'm an alcoholic, Luis. I can't drink."

"You drank when we were together before."

"I was relapsing," she said, "in more ways than one."

"What does that mean?"

"It just means I can't drink," she said.

"I could force you," he said.

"I know."

"But I won't."

"Thank you," she said, and hated saying it as soon as it was out.

"There will be more for me," he said.

He drank. She stood silently in her ridiculous dress, thinking that she could use a drink now and how it would help her courage and knowing she was lying to herself as she did it. *I won't go back*, she said to herself. *I won't be that thing again*. The monitors were playing the scenes of her captivity and their early romance. This time it played against a background of music by stringed instruments that sounded like the stuff you hear in elevators. *What a jerk*, she thought.

"Luis, my husband is a cop," she said. "Sooner or later he'll find me."

"He will not find you," Luis said.

"He will, Luis, and when he does you will be in a shitload of trouble."

Luis seemed almost serene.

"He will not find you," he said.

Chapter 7

Proctor was inland, well north of Boston, near the New Hampshire border, at a bend in the Merrimack River, where a series of falls and rapids had supplied power to the nineteenth-century textile industry, which had created the city. Before the war the city had belonged to the Yankees who ran the mills, and the French-Canadian and Irish immigrants who worked them. The Yankees had never lived there. Most of the mill management lived in company-built suburbs outside of Proctor. Now the name of the city was the only hint of its Yankee beginnings. The mills had followed the labor market to the sunbelt after the war. The Yankees had shifted gears and, without having to leave their suburbs, had clustered south in homage to the new transistor culture, an easy commute along route 128. City Hall belonged now to the Irish, the Canucks had scattered, and the rest of the city was a porridge of South and Central American immigrants.

I drove into Proctor over a bridge from south of the city, where the dirty water of the Merrimack snarled over the rapids below and churned up a yellowish foam. The mills were still there. Red brick, chain link, imposing, permanent, and largely empty. There were discount clothing outlets in some, and cut-rate furniture stores in others.

Everywhere there was graffiti—ornate, curvilinear, colorful, and defiant, on brick, on city buses, on the plywood with which windows had been boarded, on mail boxes, on billboards, swirling over the many abandoned cars, most of them stripped, some of them burned out, that decayed at the curbside. There were only Latino faces on the streets. Some old men, mostly adolescent boys, clustered on street corners and in doorways, hostile and aimless. The signs on the store fronts were in Spanish. The billboards were Spanish. The only English I saw was a sign that said: "Elect Tim Harrington, Mayor of All the People." I wondered how hard Tim was working for the Hispanic vote.

East along the river the factories thinned out, and there were tenements, three-deckers with peeling paint and no yards. The tenements gave way to big square ugly frame houses, many with asbestos shingles and aluminum siding. WPOM was about a half mile out along the river, in a squat brick building with a chain-link fence around it, next to a muffler shop. There was a ten-story transmission antenna sticking up behind it, and a big sign out front that said it was the voice of the Merrimack Valley. The gate was open and I drove in and parked in the muddy lot to the right of the station. A receptionist buzzed me in. There was a security guard with a gun in the lobby. The station's programming was playing implacably on speakers in the reception area. It was a rock station, and the music was a noise I didn't know.

The receptionist was a young woman with sadistically teased blonde hair and lime-green sneakers. The rest of her outfit seemed to be a large black bag, which she was wearing like a dress. She had a gold nose ring, and six very small gold rings in her right ear. When I came to her desk she was working on her horoscope and chewing some gum. Both. I smiled at her, about half wattage. Full wattage usually made them rip off their clothes and I didn't want this one to do that. She put down the horoscope magazine and looked up at me and chewed her gum. Both, again. Maybe I'd underestimated her.

"My name is Spenser," I said. "I'd like to talk with the station manager."

"Concerning what?" she said. Her voice sounded like a fan belt slipping.

"I'm a detective," I said. "I'm looking for someone."

"Excuse me?"

"I'm a detective, a sleuth, an investigator."

I took out my wallet and showed her my license. She stared at it blankly. It could have said "Maiden Spoiler" on it for all the difference it made to her.

"Do you have an appointment?"

"Not yet," I said. "What is the manager's name?"

"Mister Antonelli."

"Could you tell Mister Antonelli I'm here, please."

She stared at me and chewed her gum. That was two things. I knew that calling Mister Antonelli on the intercom would be one thing too many. So I waited. I was hoping she'd get through staring in a while. Nothing happened. I pointed at the intercom and smiled encouragingly.

"What was your visit concerning?"

"Lisa St. Claire," I said.

"Lisa isn't in," she said.

"And I want to know why," I said.

"You'd have to ask Mr. Antonelli about that," she said. "I just work here."

"Okay," I said. "Give him a buzz."

She nodded and picked up the phone.

"A gentleman to see you, Mister Antonelli . . . No, I don't know . . . he didn't say. He's mad because Lisa isn't here . . . Yes sir."

She hung up.

"Mister Antonelli will be out in a moment, sir."

"Thank you for your help."

The receptionist smiled like it was nothing and went back to her horoscope. I watched her while I waited for Antonelli. After a moment she stopped chewing her gum. Probably needed to concentrate.

A short, overweight guy came down the hall toward me, wearing a black-checked vest over a white shirt, which he'd buttoned to the neck. He had on black jeans and gray snakeskin cowboy boots, and he flashed a diamond ring on the little finger of his left hand that would have been worth more than the station if it were real. He was bobbing slightly to the rock music as he came toward me.

"You the one here about Lisa St. Claire?" he said.

"Yeah, Spenser, I'm a private detective."

"John Antonelli, I'm the station manager. What's the buzz on Lisa?"

"Can we go somewhere?"

"Oh yeah, sure, come on down to the office."

I followed him into the office—beige rug, ivory walls, walnut furniture, award plaques on the wall. I'd never been in a broadcaster's office that didn't have award plaques. If you were running a pro-slavery hot line, someone would probably give you an award plaque.

Antonelli sat in his swivel chair, and put one foot on an open desk drawer and tilted his chair back. Through the big window behind him I could see the full panorama of the transmission repair shop. The station on-air was grating through the speaker system into the office, though at less volume than in the lobby.

"So where's Lisa?" he said. "The other jocks have been splitting shifts to cover her. We're not a big station. We got a big audience, but we don't have a lot of stand-by people, you know?"

Antonelli smiled at me without meaning it.

"Lean and mean," he said.

"Is there a way to shut the noise off?" I said.

"You don't dig that sound? That's Rat Free, man. Group of the Year."

"Gee, they finally beat out the Mills Brothers?"

Antonelli smiled again. It was like the light in a refrigerator. On. Off.

"Kids love Rat Free," he said. "They been platinum three years in a row."

"How nice for them," I said. "Could we lose them for a few minutes while we talk?"

Antonelli shrugged. He leaned forward and turned a dial on his desk and the music faded away.

"So what's the chatter?" he said.

"Lisa left home three days ago and her whereabouts are unknown."

"She ditch the old man?"

"I don't know. Did she talk about that?"

"Lisa? No. Lisa was a very private person, you know. She never said much of anything about her personal life."

"Not even to you," I said. "So why do you think she might have ditched the old man?"

"That's what you usually think, isn't it, broad like Lisa? Real spunky, good looking, you seen her?"

"Yes."

"Girl like that, man. Most female jocks are kinda nappy, you know what I mean, that's why they're in radio. But Lisa, with those looks, man she's television stuff. I'll tell you right now, you heard it here, baby, she'll be on TV inside a year."

"Wow!" I said. "You know anything about where she worked before?"

"Not off the top, but I guess I got her résumé somewhere, she must have given me one when she applied for the job."

"That'd be good," I said.

He waited. I waited.

"You want it right now?" he said.

"Yeah."

"Might take a little while."

"I've got a little while."

"Oh sure, okay."

He picked up the phone and dialed three digits.

"Vickie? John. Yeah, could you get Lisa St. Claire's file out and bring it down to my office. Soon as you can. Thanks, doll."

While he was calling I thought how too bad it was that fashion dictated the button-up collar. His neck fleshed out over it and he looked uncomfortable, even if he wasn't. He hung up and gave me a little nod. His hair was smoothed back tight to his skull and glistened with the stuff he used to smooth it.

"She friendly with the rest of the station crew?" I said.

"She wasn't unfriendly," Antonelli said. "But they don't mingle that much. Everybody has their shift. They pass each other in the hallway, you know. Sometimes they get friendly with an engineer, or something, but Lisa wasn't much of a mixer. Tell you the truth, I think she saw this as a stepping stone. She was in ten to two, and she was gone."

"What did she do the rest of the time? Work up her music for the next day?"

Antonelli smiled.

"Naw. We work off a Top 40 service. Music's all preprogged. Most of the commercials are recorded. All Lisa had to do was a little chatter, couple live commercials, maybe a PSA, segue to the news at the top of the hour. She could come in ten minutes to ten and do all the preparation she needed."

"Challenging," I said. "What'd she get for this kind of work?"

"Salaries are confidential," Antonelli said.

"Sure," I said. "Just estimate the range for me. What's a midday disk jockey get from a station like this?"

Antonelli shrugged. "In a market like this, thirty to thirty-five K."

"Thank you."

A slim black woman with her hair in corn rows came in carrying a folder. She smiled at me, put the folder on Antonelli's desk, and went out. She had on nice perfume. Antonelli thumbed through the folder, extracted a sheet of paper, and handed it across to me. It was Lisa's résumé, dated 1992.

"May I keep this?" I said.

"I'll make a copy for you," Antonelli said. He stood, took the résumé back, copied it on a machine behind his desk, and handed me the copy.

"There you go," he said, and sat back down.

"If she left her husband, where do you think she'd go?" I said.

"Got no idea. She might go anywhere. Lisa was happening, you know. She could be around here, she could be in Vegas. I know she was taking some courses over at the college."

"Merrimack State?"

"Yeah."

"The name Tiffany mean anything to you?"

"No, except for the store."

"She friendly with any men, might have an accent?"

"Christ knows there's enough of them in Proctor. But, no, I don't know of any."

"Anybody work here named Vaughn?" I said.

"Nope."

"Know anybody named Vaughn?"

"Not that I can think of."

"If she didn't leave her husband, what other explanation might there be for her absence?" I said.

"You mean, something might have happened to her?"

"I mean, you got any thoughts on why she's not around?"

"Me? Christ, no. She just worked for me. I didn't know her well. You think something might have happened?"

"I don't know."

"I'm in a bind here," Antonelli said. "She doesn't come back, I got to hire somebody. I don't know if I should start looking now or not."

"How awful for you," I said.

"No, I don't mean, like, you know, I don't care what happens to her. But I got a station to run here, man. You know? And she's fucking me up."

I stood up and took out a business card and laid it on his desk.

"You hear anything, think of anything, call me up."

He picked up the card without looking at it.

"Yeah," he said. "Sure thing."

"Rock on," I said and went out.

She stared at him across the small table. There was candle light and the glow of the silent monitors. She stared across at him. His face was so familiar, his voice the same as it had always been, his tone light, and pleasant, slightly mocking as it always was, but calm and loving, just as she remembered. She knew he was not calm. She knew he was unstable and crazy. It was why she had left him, fled from him, really. But except that he had kidnapped her and held her prisoner, he seemed a normal man. The familiarity helped her to control the frenzy that she held back so grimly. He was, after all, the same man she'd loved. The man who had loved her, who thought he still loved her, though she knew, in the small part of her able to think, that whatever this was, it was no longer love, maybe had never been love. God, he is beautiful, she thought. I wasn't wrong about that.

"Every day will be fun, chiquita," he said. "Every day we will play a different game."

"And what's this one?" Lisa said. "Tie me up and drag me up here on a damned dolly like a pig to a barbecue?"

He laughed. "A pig at a barbecue? You. My beautiful Angela? No, I don't think so."

She put her hands on her hips and surveyed the room.

"Oh, and this is fun," she said. "A cartoon room, and cartoon costumes."

There was a table set with ornate china. There was a decanter of wine, some cheese, some fruit, some bread, just like the picnic at Crane's Beach. He gestured at the table.

"We should eat, Angel, and talk of our future."

"Future? Future? We have a past," she said. "But we don't have a goddamned future, Luis. My husband will find me, and he'll find you and he'll kill you."

"No," he said. "I think not."

"You don't know," Lisa said. "My husband . . ."

He shook his head.

"No more," he said as if to a noisy child. "He will not come. Let us have no more talk of this man. Sit down at the table."

Lisa sat. "This man will show up one day and kill you," she said. Luis smiled like an indulgent parent. Frank will come. She wasn't hungry, but she knew she should eat. I'm trying, Frank. I'm trying to stay ready. She *took some bread and a slice of cheese. She broke off a small segment of each and ate them, looking quietly at him while she chewed and swallowed. The bread seemed like Styrofoam. The cheese seemed like wax. It was difficult to swallow. Her mouth was dry and her throat was tight. Gotta eat, she thought. And broke off another piece. She took some grapes. He poured some wine from the decanter into her glass. She ignored it. The semblance of another time. The sham of intimacy was hideous. She could feel tears form behind her eyes. I want to be home with my husband, she thought. I want to be in my house. She forced herself not to cry. She would not cry! She forced a grape into her mouth and chewed it and swallowed it, squeezing it down her narrowed throat, fighting the need to wash it down with the wine.*

"That is good, Angel. It is lovely to see you eat like this. It is a good beginning."

I want to kill you, she thought.

Chapter 8

Merrimack State was a small cluster of mismatched buildings on the west fringe of Proctor, where the crime rate wasn't keeping up. It looked more like an elementary school with some outbuildings than a college. The administration building appeared once to have been a two-family house. The building had been painted white, but not recently, and the parking area out front was dirt covered. I parked in a spot marked Visitors and went in. I asked at the counter in the Registrar's Office, and got shunted around for maybe half an hour until I ended up talking to the Dean of Students.

"I know this is trying, Mister Spenser, but obviously the right to privacy is something we must respect in regard to our students."

"How about the right to get found, if they're lost?" I said.

The dean smiled politely.

"May I see your credentials, please."

I thought about showing him my gun, rejected the idea, and let him see my license.

"And you're employed by Ms. St. Claire's husband?"

"Yes."

"I'm afraid I'll need his authorization."

"Of course you do. After all, I'm asking if she's enrolled here, and if so what courses she's taking. Hot stuff like that has got to be handled discreetly."

"You may be as scornful as you wish, Mister Spenser, but it's not a question of what you're asking. There's a larger issue here."

"I think it's called self-importance."

"I beg your pardon?"

The dean's name was Fogarty. He was a small man with a trimmed beard and receding hair. He wore a business suit. He'd probably started life as a high school principal somewhere and moved up, or down, depending on your perspective. The state college system was not a hotbed of erudition.

"There is no issue here. I'm not asking you to reveal anything which is in any way of a private nature. You just like to think that whatever goes on here is weighty with high seriousness."

"Are you afraid to have me call Ms. St. Claire's husband?"

"Ms. St. Claire's husband is suffering from gunshot wounds. It will not help him to talk with a pompous asshole."

"I'm sorry. But there's no need to be offensive."

"You think I'm offensive? I'll give you offensive. Ms. Lisa St. Claire's husband is a cop. Cops look out for each other. I can, if I have to, have some really short-tempered guys from the Essex County DA's office come in here and ask you what I'm asking you. I could probably even get them to come in here in force with the sirens singing and the blue lights flashing, and haul your ass down to Salem and ask you these same questions in a holding cell."

Guys like Fogarty have power over a bunch of kids and it gets them thinking it's real, which makes them think that they're tough. It took Fogarty a minute to adjust to the fact that he was misguided in these perceptions. He stared at me with his mouth partly open, and nothing coming out.

Finally he said, "Well!"

"Well," I said.

"I don't wish to be unreasonable."

"Good."

We sat and looked at each other. Neither of us said anything.

"Well," he said again.

I looked at my watch. Fogarty picked up his phone.

"Clara, could you see if we have a student named Lisa St. Claire, please. Probably continuing education. Yes. If we do, may I have her folder? Thank you."

He hung up and looked at me and looked away.

"I guess it's why I'm an educator, Mister Spenser. I'm invested in students. Sometimes, maybe, too invested."

"Sure," I said. "That's probably it."

He was pleased that I agreed with him. He leaned back in his chair and patted his fingertips together.

"Young lives," he said. "Young lives."

A very small woman who might have been 125 shuffled in with a folder in her hand. She shuffled across the room, put the folder on Fogarty's desk, and shuffled backwards out of the room. She did not speak. She did not kiss the hem of his garment.

Fogarty picked up the folder and opened it and looked at it for a moment as if he were studying the Book of Kells. Then he raised his eyes from it and looked at me.

"Yes. Ms. St. Claire is enrolled in our continuing education program."

"What I would have called night school in my innocence," I said.

Fogarty smiled politely.

"Well, it's not really night school. Classes are held in the late afternoon and in the evening."

"What course is she taking?"

"HD31-6," he said. "Self Actualization: An Analytic Feminist Perspective."

"Yikes," I said. "What's HD stand for?"

"Human development."

"When's it meet?"

I was asking him to violate the code of *Omerta* again. He looked uncomfortable, but he rallied.

"Tuesday and Thursday, eight to nine forty-five p.m. In the Bradford Building."

"Who teaches it?"

"Professor Leighton."

"And where do I find him?"

Fogarty hesitated again.

"Pretend I'm a student, and I want to take his class. Do I stand outside and yell, 'Hey, Leighton?'"

"*Her* office is in Bradford, second floor."

"Thank you very much," I said. "Is there anything in Ms. St. Claire's folder that would shed light on where she went?"

Fogarty didn't hesitate a moment.

"Absolutely not," he said.

He'd have probably said that if there were a ransom note in there.

"And you have no thoughts on the matter?"

He shrugged in a worldly way.

"Marriages sometimes flounder," he said.

I nodded thoughtfully.

She lay on the bed in the darkness and thought about her situation. Despite the eroding intensity of her fear, she was still all right. He had not touched her. And except for tying her up when he took her, he hadn't harmed her. She wasn't home. The ordinary life rhythms she had, perhaps for the first time in her life, established, were cacophonously disrupted, but she was still whole. She was still Lisa St. Claire. She thought of her husband. She knew he would find her. Sooner or later, no matter what, Frank would come. She missed him. She wanted more than she had ever wanted anything to see him. To see the door to this black room open and to see Frank walk through it. She had never been altogether sure she loved him. She liked sex with him. But she liked sex. If she were to be totally objective, she would probably say it wasn't better with Frank than others. With Luis, before, in fact, the wildness of it, the adventure of it, might have made sex with Luis a little better than sex with anyone. Frank had been the one she fled to after she fled Luis. And more than Luis, when she fled all that she had been. Frank had been calmness and stability and probably above all else safety. A tough cop. He would keep her secure. He would keep her whole. He would protect her from what she had been and from what she always feared she might be again. In his calmness and his clarity and his strength he was a stay against disintegration. It was ironic really, if she could detach herself, that the kidnapping had dispelled the last of the romantic vapors that had clung retrospectively to Luis. Now and then at breakfast in their upscale kitchen, quietly, ready to go to work, she would remember Luis and wonder if there might be something there that she shouldn't have abandoned—infinite possibility, maybe, music from beyond a distant hill, something like that. There had been an I-don't-give-a-damn excitement about Luis that Lisa occasionally remembered with nostalgia as she watched her husband eat the same breakfast he always ate. She liked him. He was good for her. But she had sometimes wondered, as her mind rolled over her life before him, if she had made a mistake. She knew she hadn't. She knew what Luis was, and even more, she knew what Luis represented for her. But often, in a sort of visceral way, she wondered about Luis. Now I do not, she thought. Now more than anything I have ever wanted, I want him to find me and take me home. It was more than the corrosive fear that made her long for her *husband. It was what he was and what he represented—a life to be lived, a connection to be nurtured, a full chance to be Lisa St. Claire. He'll come, she thought. He'll find me. And alone in the dark lying on the alien bed she cried for the first time since Luis took her.*

Chapter 9

Rowena Leighton was small and slender and dark, with her dark hair pulled back in a French twist, and her big dark eyes made darker with mascara, and bigger by the lenses of her large round glasses. The glasses had blue and gold frames. She wore a loose yellow pants suit with a wide black belt, and black high-heeled shoes with laces and clunky heels like the Wicked Witch of the West used to wear. There were rings on most of her fingers, and large ornamental earrings in her ears. Her face was thin and her jaw line firm. Her lipstick was very loud and generously applied to a mouth that seemed as if, in its natural state, it would be kind of thin. It was an intense, intelligent face and at the moment it was nearly buried in a book titled *Modes of Being: The Tactical Personae of Men and Women in the Modern World.* Professor Leighton was carefully marking things with a yellow highlighter. I waited. She continued to mark.

I smiled courteously and said, "My name is Spenser. I'm a detective, and I'm looking for Lisa St. Claire, who appears to be missing." She kept marking and I held the courteous smile until she finally looked up and saw it.

Charmed by the smile she said, "Dean Fogarty called to say you might come by. What's this about Lisa?"

"She a student of yours?" I said.

"Yes. Very gifted."

The office was cluttered with the detritus of scholarship. There were books piled everywhere, and manila folders spilling papers on the top of a long mission oak table under the windows. A Macintosh word processor sat on a corner of her desk, hooked to a laser printer on a small end table beside her.

"And you teach a class in self-actualization?" I said.

"A workshop, actually, for women in process," Professor Leighton said. "It's based on some of the transactional theories I've developed in my work."

She gestured slightly with her head to indicate a cluster of five books on one shelf of her book case. They had been set aside and held upright by a pair of used bricks. I could see her name on the spine of each. I couldn't read the titles without turning my head parallel to the floor. That position is never my best look, so I passed on the titles.

"Tell me about Lisa?" I said.

"You're a detective?"

"Yes."

"A police detective?"

"No, private."

"Really? How fascinating. Have you always been a private detective?"

"No, once I was a police detective."

"And were you discharged?"

"Yes."

"Dishonestly?"

"No, they felt I was rebellious."

She leaned back in her chair and laughed. It was a real laugh.

"I didn't know intellectuals did that," I said.

"Laugh? Oh, I think real intellectuals do. Remember, life is a tragedy to those who feel, but a comedy to those who think."

"Horace Walpole?" I said.

"Oh my," she said. "A learned detective. Did you enjoy Dean Fogarty?"

"Uneasy lies the head that wears a Deanship," I said.

She laughed again.

"Well, you are a delight. Yes, Dean Fogy, as we call him, has never taken himself lightly."

"Was it Horace Walpole?" I said.

"Oh hell, I don't know. I think it was. Certainly you're in the right century. How can I help you with Lisa?"

"Did she have a friend in your class named Tiffany?"

"Yes," Professor Leighton smiled. "Typhanie Hall. She spelled her first name T-y-p-h-a-n-i-e. She wished to be an actress."

"Talk to me about Lisa, what was she like, who her friends were."

"Well, of course I am limited by the artificialities of the student-teacher relationship. Clearly she was a bright woman. Clearly she had damn good insights about human interaction—she may have had some psychotherapy. And clearly she was not very well educated. She was some sort of radio personality, so she'd learned how to speak smoothly and she was facile and charming and attractive, all of which might mislead one at first, but it became quickly apparent that she'd had little formal schooling."

Professor Leighton smiled at me.

"You would notice it promptly," she said.

"I did," I said.

"In some ways I would say she is the opposite of you. You speak like a hooligan, but you know a great deal."

"I am a hooligan," I said. "I read a lot."

"Apparently. Do you fear, ah, for lack of a better word, foul play? Or is she simply a wandering wife?"

"You knew she was married?"

"She wore a ring."

"But she kept, whatever the proper phrase is now, the name she had when she was single," I said.

"You can relax, Mister Spenser, I am not one of your bushy feminist theoreticians. I accept 'maiden name' as a useful locution. In fact, I have always used my maiden name."

"You're married?"

"Thrice," she said with a smile. "None of them current. I guess I'm a bit rebellious myself."

"Good you used the maiden name then," I said. "Be a Chinese fire drill to keep changing it every time."

"Plan ahead," she said. "Is she in harm's way, or merely adventuring?"

"I don't know," I said. "A few days after she disappeared, her husband was shot."

"Did he survive?" Professor Leighton said.

"Yes."

"Is she a suspect?"

"I don't suspect her. But I'm not trying to catch the shooter. I'm looking for Lisa."

"Was it Luis?"

"Was who Luis?" I said. Cagey.

"Did she marry Luis Deleon?"

"No. She married a Boston cop named Frank Belson. Who's Luis Deleon?"

"He was a student of mine last year, in my evening seminar on Media and Identity. Lisa St. Claire was in that class as well. I believe they enrolled together. They were very friendly, intimately so."

"You know this?"

"I can't prove it. I know it."

"By observation?"

"By observation. They sat together, they giggled together like much younger people. They clung together in the hall during the break. They held hands. They whispered. I've been in love, or infatuated, or both many times. I know it when I see it."

"Tell me about Luis," I said. "Is he Hispanic?"

"Yes, from Proctor, and like many Hispanics in Proctor, I fear he is very poor. The college runs an outreach program for the disadvantaged, as they like to call them. It sets aside a certain number of scholarships for the community and Luis took advantage of one of them."

"How old?"

"Luis? A bit younger than Lisa, perhaps, say twenty-six, twenty-seven."

"Does he have an accent?"

"Not very much, enough to discern, but nothing to impede communication."

"What else?" I said.

"Luis, like Lisa, was very bright, but very uneducated. Most of what he knew, that was germane to my classroom, he learned from television and movies. I am not entirely sure he knew where film ended and life began."

" 'Germane to my classroom'?" I said. "Why the qualifier?"

"Because I have some sense that he knows many things about life in the Proctor barrio that I cannot even dream of."

"Is he in any of your classes this year?"

"No. I'm a visiting professor here so I can do some postdoctoral study at Brandeis. This is my one class of the semester."

"He still enrolled at the college?"

"I don't know. Dean Fogy can tell you. I don't believe he was entirely comfortable in an Anglo academic setting, even this one."

"He ever come around to see Lisa before class or after?"

"Not this year."

"Any observations you've made on Luis you'd like to share?"

"In some ways he was quite formidable. Very tall. Athletic looking."

"How tall?"

"Unusually tall. Taller by several inches than you. Though not perhaps as thick. How tall are you?"

"Six one."

She looked at me appraisingly for a moment.

"He was probably six feet four or five," she said. "Very intense, full of machismo. I know that is said of many Latin men, but Luis did tend to strut."

She leaned back a little and closed her big eyes behind her huge glasses and thought for a moment.

"And yet he was also very innocent," she said. "He believed in absolutes, in the kind of world you see in television movies. Good is always good. Bad is always bad. Nothing is very complicated, and what is once is forever. He imagined the kind of life that one would imagine if one grew up staring at television. No experience seemed to shake that imaginative conceit."

"You wouldn't know where he lives?"

"No, I'm sorry. I guess I'll have to refer you once again to dear Dean Fogy. The college must have an address."

"Anyone named Vaughn in Lisa's class?"

"Not that I recall."

"You know anyone named Vaughn?"

She smiled.

"There was a baseball player named Arky Vaughn," she said.

"Yes there was," I said. "Pirates and Dodgers. Probably not our man."

"Horace Walpole *and* Arky Vaughn," she said. "I *am* impressed."

I gave her my card.

"If there's anything else that you think of, no matter how inconsequential, please call me."

"I'll be pleased to," she said.

I started for the door and stopped and turned back.

"I have met a number of professors," I said. "And none of them were notable for honesty, humor, lack of pretense, and ability to observe. What the hell are you doing here?"

She smiled at me for a moment and then said, "I came for the waters."

"There are no waters here," I said.

"I was misinformed," she said.

Chapter 10

The dean had given me Typhanie Hall's address, which was in Cambridge, and Luis Deleon's, which was, improbably, in Marblehead. Cambridge was closer, and I had a suspicion that Marblehead was going to be a waste of time, so here I was with an appointment to see Typhanie on a bright sunny morning. Crocuses were up, and the Harvard students were out in all their infinite variety. I waited in my car on Brattle Street while two Episcopalian women wearing big hats and Nike running shoes paused in the middle of the road to discuss human rights. I wanted to run them over. Cambridge was the jay-walking capital of the world, and I felt the only way to get control of the situation would be to kill a few. I was, however, wary of the Cambridge Police, so I blew my horn instead. The ladies looked up and glared at me. One, wearing purple stockings and sandals, gave me the finger.

I didn't like where the Lisa St. Claire thing was going, but I wasn't in charge of where it went. So when the ladies got out of the way, I parked near Longfellow Park under a sign that said Resident Parking Only, and found Typhanie Hall's address, down a side street, near Mt. Auburn.

Typhanie had an apartment with a side entrance on the first floor of a large yellow Victorian house. When she let me in she was wearing aquamarine spandex tights and an oversized navy blue tee shirt. Her bright yellow hair was pulled back and held in place with one of those frilly elastic dinguses designed for the purpose. A long pony tail spilled down her back.

She had on a lot of eye shadow, and her nails were long and brilliant red. Like, wow!

"Do you have any word on Lisa?" she said when I was in and seated on a big hassock in her blond wood living room.

"Not really," I said. "You?"

"No. I'm worried to death about her. Ordinarily we talk nearly every day."

"You have no idea where she might go?"

"Maybe her dad," Typhanie said. "She always talked about visiting her dad."

"You know where her dad might be?"

"No."

"You know his name?"

"No."

"Is his last name St. Claire?"

"I don't know. She always said she wanted to find him, but she would never talk about him. Would you like some coffee? Or tea?"

"No thanks."

A big yellow cat came around the corner and sniffed at my foot and then rubbed himself along my leg.

"That's Chekov," she said. "He's usually not that friendly with strangers. You must be special. You don't mind if I have some coffee, do you?"

I shook my head.

"I'm just not anything at all without several cups in the morning to get my motor revved."

Her motor seemed sufficiently revved to me, but I had just met her and didn't know what kind of rev she was capable of. I waited while she went to the kitchen and came back with her coffee in a large white mug. The mug had a picture of Einstein on the side.

"You've known Lisa for a long time?" I said.

The yellow cat lay on his back on the floor by my foot and looked at me with his oval yellow eyes nearly shut. I rubbed his ribs with the toe of my shoe a little and he purred.

"Oh yes, we met last fall, at the Cambridge Center Adult Ed center. We both love taking classes. Both of us love a good time, and we hit it right off. Would you like some Perrier or some spring water?"

"No thank you. Did she date a lot?"

"Oh yes. We both did. I'm not one of those grim feminists. I love men."

"You're not?" I said.

Typhanie smiled brilliantly.

"She go with anyone in particular?"

"Well, she was dating Luis. But Lisa wasn't ready to settle down, in those days. She was looking for a good time."

"Until she met Belson," I said.

"Yes, then it was time."

"Why?"

"Why?"

I realized I couldn't move too swiftly with Typhanie.

"Yeah, why was it time?" I said.

"Who knows? There's a time for everything, you know? Before then it wasn't time. Then it was."

"Of course," I said.

"I really believe that," Typhanie said. "Don't you? That timing is pretty much everything in life? And Frank came along at the right time for Lisa, and pow!"

The cat on the floor had turned onto its side and stretched itself as long as it could get. It reached up with one paw and batted at my pants leg.

"What made it the right time?" I said.

"Who can say? The relationship with Luis wasn't going the way she wanted, and then here came this older man, you know? A safe harbor in a storm."

"Luis Deleon?" I said.

"Yes." Typhanie gave me what she must have thought was a wicked smile. "Her Latin lover."

"She was going with him when she met Belson?"

"Yes."

"Tell me about him."

"Well, he's beautiful. He's Hispanic, from Proctor. She met him in a night class at Merrimack State. Lisa was taking some courses there, nights, you know. She didn't want to always be a disc jockey."

"And they were, ah, lovers?"

"Oh baby, you better believe it. They were a continuing explosion. Everything was passionate like you dream about, you know, like in the movies. Flowers and candy and champagne and midnight suppers and, well, I shouldn't be telling tales out of school, but, honey, they were hot."

"Sex?"

"Everywhere, all the time, according to Lisa."

"How nice," I said. "So what happened? How come she ended up with Frank Belson?"

"I don't know. It was awful sudden. I know that Luis was pushing her to marry him."

"And she didn't want to?"

Typhanie shook her head.

"Why not?" I said.

"I don't know, really. I mean, he was younger than she was, and he was, you know, Hispanic, and I don't know what kind of job he had. But boy, he was compelling. Looks. Charm."

She shrugged.

"On the other hand, boy toy is one thing," Typhanie said. "Husband's a whole different ball game."

"You married?" I said.

"Not right now," Typhanie said. "You?"

"No."

"Ever been married?"

"No."

"You gay?"

"No."

"With someone?"

"Yeah."

"I shoulda stayed with my second husband. Now every time I meet somebody interesting they're either taken or gay. You fool around?"

"No. But if I did I'd call you first. The name Vaughn mean anything to you?"

"Stevie Ray Vaughn," she said hopefully.

"Un huh," I said. "You know where Luis Deleon is now?"

She shrugged.

"Proctor, I imagine."

"You know what he does?"

"Like for a living?"

"Un huh."

"No, I never did know. I always kind of wondered."

"Why?"

"He seemed to have money, but he never said anything about his job."

"What'd he talk about when you were with him?"

"Lisa, theater, movies. He loved movies. Had a video camera. Always had a video camera."

"You wouldn't have a picture, would you?"

"Of Luis? No, I don't think so. I'm not one for keeping stuff, pictures and all that. I just keep right on moving, you know?"

"How is Luis's English? He speak with an accent?"

"He speaks very well, only a slight hint of an accent, really."

The yellow cat rolled over and onto his feet and padded away from me to a plaid upholstered rocker across the room and jumped up in it and curled up and went to sleep.

"Thanks," I said.

I took a card out of my pocket and gave it to her.

"If you hear anything or think of anything, please call me."

"You don't think anything bad has happened, do you?"

"I don't know what has happened," I said.

"What are you going to do now?"

"I'm going to go find Luis Deleon," I said.

Typhanie's eyes widened.

"Because of what I told you?"

"Because of what a couple people have told me," I said.

"Don't tell him I said anything."

"Okay."

"Luis is, ah, kind of scary," Typhanie said.

"Scary how?" I said.

"He's so passionate, so . . . quick. I wouldn't want to make him mad."

"Me either," I said. "But you never know."

He had not touched her yet. She didn't know if he would. He had her. He could force her. Why would he not? What he felt for her wasn't love. She knew that. But maybe there was love in it. Maybe it kept him from forcing her. Yet, of course, he was forcing her. Forcing her to be here. Forcing her to wear his stupid outfits and live in this cartoon set of a room. Still he had not forced her sexually. And he had not physically hurt her. The air-conditioning hummed, the monitors played. The sound track was on and she heard herself again and again giggling at the beach, struggling in the back of the truck. There was no way for her to tell time. No light, no dark except as he turned the lights on and off, no television except the mocking images of her own bondage, no radio, no clocks. She saw only him, and now and then the young-faced serving woman who never spoke. The food offered her no clues; what she ate was not specific to any meal, and she wondered if it were deliberate on his part, a kind of brainwashing. It underscored how captive she was. She could not choose to eat. She had to wait to be fed. Or was it simply a part of how she knew he was enveloped in make-believe, creating still another artificial environment, pretending to be a bandit prince, pretending to be her lover. She felt the shame of her situation, how she had so freely taken up with this man, so carelessly put aside what she had learned so painfully in California, knowing as she felt the shame that it was not a matter of shame, that she had been drawn to him by needs she hadn't yet mastered, as she had drunk with him, before she mastered that once more as well. And she would master this. He would not pull her back down. She had been too far down. She had struggled too painfully up. She had lapsed again and escaped again and she would escape this. She wouldn't go back. She would be Lisa St. Claire. She was Lisa St. Claire, and because she was she was also Mrs. Frank Belson. Frank would find her.

Chapter 11

I started at Proctor Police Headquarters. It was a gray granite building, near the gray granite City Hall. It had been built in the British Imperial style of the nineteenth century when a lot of American public buildings were being erected by people filled with swagger and destiny. It had been shiny and new once, when the WASPs ran the city, and the mills pumped money into everyone's pockets. But now it was hunched and crumbled like the city, buckling beneath the weight of impoverishment. There was graffiti on most of the walls, and litter washed up against the gray stone foundation. The windows were covered with wire mesh, and one of the glass panels in the front door had been broken and replaced with unpainted plywood. It looked like it wasn't exterior plywood either, because it had already begun to blister in the damp spring air, and the ends were starting to separate.

There was a sign on the duty officer's desk in the high lobby. It said Officer McDonogh. Behind the sign, seated at the desk, reading a newspaper, was a fat cop with his tie down and the neck of his uniform blouse unbuttoned. He seemed to be sweating a lot even though it wasn't hot, and he had a white handkerchief tied around his neck. A cigarette sent a small blue twist of smoke up from the edge of the desk, where it rested among the burn marks.

I said, "You McDonogh?"

He looked up from his paper, as if the question were a hard one, stared at me for a minute, and shook his head.

"Naw. Sign's been there since the war. What do you want?"

"Billy Kiley still Chief of Detectives?" I said.

"Naw, Kiley retired three, four years ago. Delaney's Chief now. You know Kiley?"

He picked up the cigarette, spilled some ash on his belly, and took a drag.

"I used to," I said, "when I was working for the Middlesex DA."

"Well, he's gone. You want to see Delaney?"

"Yes."

The fat cop jerked his head down the corridor behind him.

"Last door," he said and picked up the phone as I walked away.

The corridor had once been marble, and some of it still showed above the green painted Sheetrock that had been layered onto the lower walls like an ugly wainscotting. Thread-bare brown carpet covered the floor. The corridor was long and on each side of it were pebbled glass doors with the names of the occupants stenciled on the glass. Identification and Forensic. Traffic. Juvenile. Delaney's office was at the end, a big one, with palladian windows on two sides. The ceilings were high. There were a couple of yellow oak file cabinets on the wall to my right. Near the left wall, a conference table was littered with crumpled Coke cans, overturned Styrofoam coffee cups, some ash trays full of cigarette butts, and the faint traces of powdered sugar where someone had polished off a donut. Beyond the conference table was the half-ajar door to a private washroom. I smiled when I saw it. They don't build them this way anymore. Delaney was just putting the phone down when I came in. He looked a little surprised, as if people didn't come in very often.

"My name's Spenser," I said.

"So, what's the Middlesex DA want with me?" Delaney said. He was a tallish man, gone soft, with a lot of broken blood vessels in his cheeks, and an ugly red vinyl hairpiece on top of his head. It didn't match his sideburns, but it probably wouldn't have matched anyone's sideburns except maybe Plastic Man's. He or the guy out front had confused the part about I-used-to-work-for-the-Middlesex-DA. I decided not to clarify it.

"Looking for information on a guy named Luis Deleon."

"You try 411?" Delaney smiled. He had big yellow teeth like a horse.

"He's not in the phone book," I said.

"Why you asking about him?"

"Missing persons case I'm on," I said. "Woman named Lisa St. Claire. I thought Deleon might know something about her."

"Why do you think that?"

"She's married now to somebody else, but they used to date."

"He a Cha Cha?"

"Yeah."

"She's Anglo?"

"Un huh."

Delaney shook his head. He glanced over toward the washroom and then glanced back at me.

"You think she's with him?"

"I don't know," I said. "I just thought I'd talk with him. See what he knew. You ever hear of him?"

"Deleon don't even sound spic, does it? Doesn't matter. Fucking cucarachas change their name around here every other day."

He looked at the washroom again and licked his lips.

"You wanna excuse me," he said. "Got to use the facilities for a minute."

"Sure."

He got up and headed for the lav. The door closed. I heard him cough, a deep ugly sound, then some silence. Then the flush of the toilet. The door opened and Delaney came out. He looked calmer, and as he passed me on the way to his desk, I smelled the booze on him. He sat down at his desk, his eyes bright. Booze was what he'd gone to the lavatory for. The toilet flush was just camouflage.

"So you think some spic's got your girl," he said.

I shook my head.

"I don't know if anyone's got the woman," I said. "She may be in Augusta, Georgia, for all I know, listening to Ray Charles records. You got any paper on this guy Deleon?"

"Paper? You mean like a rap sheet? Like a record?"

Delaney laughed and the laugh turned into a cough and he coughed until he had to spit in his handkerchief. Still coughing, with his handkerchief pressed to his mouth, he stood and went back into the lav. He was gone a couple of minutes and when he came back he was carrying a bottle of Bushmill's Irish Whiskey. He sat down and put the whiskey on the desk near him.

"Fucking cough," he said when he got himself back to breathing. "Whiskey's only thing that'll stop it. You want a pop?"

"No thanks," I said.

Delaney took a Styrofoam cup from the side table by his desk and blew in it to clear the dust and poured maybe three inches of whiskey into the cup. He drank some. He downed about half of it and licked his lips. His eyes were bright now, and his face, reddened with broken veins, was brighter red.

"Ahh," Delaney said. "Mother's milk."

I knew the feeling. I'd never been a drunk, but I'd drunk enough to know the feeling, the sense of well-being as the whiskey eased through your system. It was a feeling that was hard to keep balanced and Delaney had the look of a man for whom it was getting harder. Keep the buzz without getting so drunk you couldn't function. It could be done, and Delaney was sort of doing it, living a life of never quite drunk and never at all sober, nursing the bottle in hidden sips until he got to the point where he couldn't hide the sips. It was no longer pleasure for him. It was need. Booze was no longer recreation. It was medicine.

"Where was I?" Delaney said.

"I asked if you had any record on Luis Deleon, and you laughed so hard you started coughing, and coughed so hard you started to spit up and then you went and got your bottle and now you're happy. You got any record on Luis Deleon?"

"What is this, spic fucking central? They all got records, and they all got twenty names and fifty addresses. You want to find out about some spic in Proctor, you talk to Freddie Santiago, or you go over to San Juan Hill. That's where it's happening for all the spics around here, man, Freddie or San Juan Hill. That's spic central, pal."

He drank the rest of his whiskey. And poured himself some more.

"Tell me about San Juan Hill," I said.

The whiskey was making him expansive. He leaned back in his chair. The bottle on the table now, no more pretense. He eyed the bottle. It was a new one, nearly full. He was able to relax. He knew where the next drink was.

"The spics are divided into two factions. One of them is San Juan Hill, the other one is Freddie Santiago."

"Is San Juan Hill a place?"

"Yeah, north end of the city. It used to be Irish and when it was we called it Galway Bay. My mother was born there. Then the Cha Chas came in and we moved out and now it's San Juan Hill."

"And Freddie Santiago?"

"Guy runs a place called Club del Aguadillano in the south end of town. He's the establishment, you know what I mean, sort of a spic Godfather. Kids in San Juan Hill broke with him maybe five, six years ago, and we don't know how organized they are, but you're in San Juan Hill, you're on the other side of whatever fight Freddie's in."

He sipped some more whiskey, held it in his mouth, then tilted his head and let it trickle down his throat.

"You got anybody in there?"

"Anybody in where?"

"In San Juan Hill, in with Freddie Santiago."

"Shit no, man, Anglo won't last ten minutes under cover with one of the spic outfits, fuckers don't even speak English, most of them."

"I was thinking you might have some Hispanic officers."

Delaney laughed, started to cough, and swallowed some whiskey. The coughing subsided.

"His-pan-ic officers?" he started to laugh, caught himself, and drank again. "You think we're going to give one of those assholes a badge and a gun? They'd pawn the badge to buy dope and stick up the pawn shop afterwards."

"Any Spanish-speaking officers on the force?"

"Shit no. Freddie speaks English. We get along good with Freddie."

"I'll bet you do," I said.

Delaney paid no attention.

"Freddie's a businessman," Delaney said. "Runs a tight ship."

There was admiration in Delaney's voice.

"Gets a lot of dope and pussy traffic from the prep-school kids come in from Andover, and he don't want to scare them away. Walk around the south end, the streets are clean, the street lights work. There's zero street crime in Freddie's area."

"How about San Juan Hill?"

Delaney shook his head.

"Dodge City," he said. "Bunch of coked-up gang bangers. All we can do is pen them in up there, keep it on the Hill."

"You think Deleon might be connected to Santiago?"

"Deleon." Delaney shook his head, fumbled on the desk for his bottle, poured a little more into his Styrofoam cup.

"What kind of fucking Spanish name is that? De-le-fucking-on?"

"Probably one of Ponce's offspring," I said.

"Well I don't know nothing about him."

"Could he be on San Juan Hill?"

"Sure, he could be up there, pal. Fucking Elvis could be up there singing 'You ain't nothing but a hound dog,' you know?"

"Think Freddie Santiago would know?"

"Got no way of knowing, pal. Whyn't you go ask him?"

"Probably will," I said.

"You better ask nice, state cop or no."

"I'm not a state cop."

"You said . . ."

"I said I used to work for the Middlesex DA. I don't anymore. I'm private."

"Private? A fucking shoofly? Get the fuck out of here before I bust you for impersonating a police officer."

"Or vice versa," I said.

"Beat it," he said.

I took his advice, and as I went out the door I looked back and smiled a friendly smile and said "Skol!" and closed the door behind me.

The fat cop at the desk was still sweating as I passed him.

"How is he?" he said.

"Gassed," I said.

The cop nodded.

"He wasn't a bad cop, once," the cop said.

"He's a bad cop now," I said.

The fat cop shrugged.

"His brother's a City Councilman," he said.

Chapter 12

San Juan Hill, when I found it, made you think maybe God liked cinema noir. The streets were narrow and the three-deckers crowded down against them. The buildings were uniformly stoop-shouldered and out of plumb, as if age and sequential squalor had sapped the strength from the wooden framing. The buildings were immediately on the sidewalk, there were no yards. There was no grass or trees, no shrubs, not even weeds, pushing up through the asphalt. Between each building was a hot-topped driveway, some with new cars parked there, some with rusting hulks that had been parked there since San Juan Hill was Galway Bay. The graffiti was intense, and brilliant; an angry, aggressive plaint of garish color on almost every surface. Somebody see me! Anybody! A swarm of young kids on mountain bikes flashed out of an alley and swooped by me. One of them scraped something, probably a 20d nail head, along the length of my car as he passed. I thought about shooting him, decided it could be construed as overreaction, and chose instead to ignore it in a dignified manner. I wondered how these impoverished children could afford bright new mountain bikes. Depended, I supposed, on one's priorities. There were trash cans out on every corner, but no sign that the city had been by to pick them up. Many had been tipped over, probably by the fun-loving kids on the mountain bikes, and the trash was scattered on the sidewalks and into the street. There were dogs nosing in the trash. They were mostly the kind of generic mongrel that seems to have bred itself back to the origin of the species, twenty, thirty pounds, gray-brown, with a tail that curled upward over their hindquarters. They were so similar they looked like a breed. They all had the low-slung furtive movements of feral animals. None of them looked friendly. Most of them looked like they didn't eat regularly. And what they did eat they probably foraged. The shades in all the windows appeared to be drawn. There were a lot of kids on the streets, but very few people over the age of twenty. Occasionally there was a storefront with hand-painted Spanish language signs in the window. *Comidas, cervezas.* Most of the kids had on colorful warmup jackets, and baggy jeans and expensive sneakers. Probably traded the mountain bikes in on the sneakers as they passed through puberty. Under the weak spring sun, the graffiti, the warmup clothes, and the sneakers were nearly the only colors in San Juan Hill. Everything else was the color of the dogs.

Near the center of San Juan Hill stood an ugly pile of angular gray stones which had blackened with time. It was a Roman Catholic church with a wide wooden door painted red. The door and most of the church walls were ornamented with graffiti. There was a sign out front that identified the church as St. Sebastian's, and listed the scheduled masses. The sign was covered with graffiti. I parked out front of the church. In San Juan Hill you could park anywhere.

Inside the church, in the back, there were three old women wearing black shawls over their heads. I had read somewhere that the Catholic church no longer required women to cover their heads when entering, but these did not look like women who would jump onto every new fad that came along. The women were saying the rosary, their lips moving silently, fingering the beads softly, sliding them along as they said the prayers. Down front a solitary old man in a black suit with no tie and his white shirt buttoned to the neck was sitting in the first pew. He didn't show any signs of prayer. He wasn't sleeping. He simply sat gazing straight ahead.

As I walked down the aisle of the church, a middle-aged priest in a black cassock came out of the sacristy and met me near the altar rail.

"May I help you?" he said softly.

He was a modest-sized guy, wiry and trim with white hair and a red face.

"Is there someplace we can talk, Father?"

The priest nodded.

"Perhaps we can step out onto the front steps," he said, "so as not to disturb the worshipers."

We walked back up the central aisle in the dim, candle-smelling church, and out into the thin early spring brightness. At the foot of the church stairs my car sat at the curb, a long scratch gleaming newly along the entire passenger side. The priest looked at it.

"Your car?" he said.

"Yes."

"Welcome to San Juan Hill," the priest said. "Children on bicycles?"

"Yes."

"They like to do that," the priest said. "They particularly like to surround Anglo women, and when the car stops to beat them."

"Because they like to?"

"Because they like to."

"Sure," I said. "I'm looking for a young man named Luis Deleon. He might be here in San Juan Hill."

"Why are you looking for him?"

"As a means to an end," I said. "There's a woman missing, I'm looking for her. I'm told she once had a relationship with Deleon."

"Is this an Anglo woman?"

"Yes."

"You would not bother to look for a Latin woman."

"I look for anyone I'm hired to look for."

"You are not a policeman then?"

"No. I'm a private detective."

"And you have a gun," the priest said, "under your coat."

"You're very observant, Father."

"I have seen a lot of guns, my friend," the priest said.

"Yes, I imagine you have," I said.

The priest looked out over the gray and graffiti landscape of Proctor. Somewhere a car squealed its tires as it went at high speed around a corner. In the asphalt and chain-link playground across from the church, three kids sat against the wall smoking, and drinking from a wine bottle in a paper sack. A huge dirty gray cat, slouched so low that its belly dragged, padded out of the alley next to the church carrying a dead rat.

"Not what I imagined when I left the seminary thirty years ago," the priest said. "Bright, fresh-scrubbed children gazing up at me, learning the word of God. Green lawn in front of the church, bean suppers in the basement, young couples getting married, solemn funerals for prosperous old people who had died quietly in their sleep."

The priest looked at me.

"I was supposed to live a life of reverence," he said. "I was supposed to visit suburban hospitals, where the staff knew and admired me, and give communion to people in flowery bed linens, with bows in their hair."

"The ways of the Lord are often dark, but never pleasant, Father."

"Who said that?"

"Besides me? A guy named Reich, I think."

"I don't know him. I hope he is not correct."

"You know Deleon?" I said.

"Yes."

"You know where I can find him?"

"No, I have not seen him since he was small. His mother used to bring him, then, but she was a desperate woman and one day she killed herself, God rest her soul. I never saw Luis again. But I hear things. I hear he has become an important person in San Juan Hill."

The priest paused and looked at me.

"And I hear he has become very dangerous."

I nodded.

"You should be careful if you plan to approach him," the priest said.

"I'm fairly dangerous myself, Father."

"Yes, you have the look. I have seen it far too often not to know it."

"If you were me, Father, where would you look for Deleon?"

"I don't know."

"Would any of your parishioners know?"

"If they do, they would not tell me."

"You're their priest."

"Here I am not their priest. I am a gringo."

I nodded. The priest was silent. I could hear a boom box playing some-where.

"If you do not speak Spanish, no one in San Juan Hill will speak with you."

"Even if they speak English?"

"Even then."

"How about Freddie Santiago?" I said.

"He might speak to you, if he thought it served him. But he is not in San Juan Hill."

"What would serve Santiago?" I said.

The priest thought about my question.

"There is no simple answer to that," he said. "Santiago is an evil man, of this there is no question. He is a criminal, almost surely a murderer. He deals in narcotics, in prostitutes, in gambling. He sells green cards. He con-trols much of what happens in the Hispanic community here, which is to say most of Proctor."

"Except San Juan Hill," I said.

"Except San Juan Hill."

"So what's the no-simple part?"

"He is not entirely, I think, a bad man. A poor person can get money or a job from Freddie Santiago. Wars among some of the youth gangs are settled by him. Paternity and alimony payments are often enforced by him. Every election he works very hard to get Hispanic people registered."

"And he probably contributes to the Police Beneficent Association," I said.

The priest smiled for a moment.

"I think it is certain," he said, "that Freddie Santiago contributes generously to the police. Have you talked to them?"

"I talked to the Chief of Detectives," I said.

"He was Irish?" the priest said.

"Yeah, Delaney."

"They are all Irish," the priest said. "The police, the school superintendent, the mayor, all of the power structure. They are Irish and they speak English. And the city is Spanish and speaks Spanish."

"You speak Spanish, Father?"

"Haltingly at best," the priest said. "I can still say a Latin mass, but I have not been successful with the language of my flock. I assume the police weren't helpful to you."

"They weren't."

"If she's with Deleon . . . an Anglo woman with an Hispanic man . . . for the police here, it would mean she was irretrievably tainted."

Six teenaged boys in baggy jeans and San Antonio Spurs warmup jackets swaggered by us on the sidewalk below. They looked up at us. It was not a friendly look. One of them said something in Spanish. They all laughed.

"Did you understand what he said?" I asked the priest.

"He said, in effect, 'Look at the eunuch in his dress,'" the priest said. His red face held no expression. "I've heard it before."

"If they would talk to me, is there enough English spoken in Proctor for me to ask questions and understand the answers?" I said.

"They will not talk to you, and if they would, I do not think they could," the priest said.

"But Freddie Santiago speaks English," I said.

"Very well, I've heard. If you talk to him, be respectful, and very careful. He is a deadly adversary."

"Wait'll he gets a load of me," I said. "How'd you end up here, Father, in the tail end of hell's half acre?"

"A priest's duty is to serve where God sends him," he said.

As he spoke, he was looking at the barren asphalt playground where the three kids were still drinking wine and smoking dope against the graffiti-covered handball wall.

"And . . . I drink," he said.

Chapter 13

Quirk came into my office like he always does, like it was his, and don't argue about it. He was wearing a tan suit and a blue-striped shirt with a button-down collar and a khaki-colored knit tie. It was as springlike as the weather, which was soft and flowery with a slight breeze drifting in through the open window. He pulled one of my client chairs around and sat down and put one foot on my desk.

"What have you got?" Quirk said.

"There's a guy named Luis Deleon," I said.

"Yeah."

"He's an Hispanic guy from Proctor who Lisa met in a class at Merrimack State."

"Un huh."

"Apparently Lisa had a relationship with him, before she met Belson."

"Un huh."

"You been listening to her answering machine tapes?" I said.

"Yeah. Guy has maybe a little Spanish accent, on the tape. Says he's going to stop by."

"Could be Deleon," I said.

"And?"

"He lives in a section of Proctor called San Juan Hill," I said. "I've talked to some people. He's sort of a figure there. Wrong side of the law, I think. The way I hear it, Deleon may also be on the wrong side of the local Godfather, Freddie Santiago."

"Santiago's got a lot of juice in Proctor," Quirk said. "You speak any Spanish?"

"No," I said.

"You know where this guy Deleon is?"

"No. San Juan Hill someplace, but we don't have an address yet."

"We probably ought to get one," Quirk said.

"She may not be with him."

"Sure," Quirk said. "But it's the best lead you got. What are you waiting for?"

"If Lisa's with Deleon, voluntarily or involuntarily, we need to go a little careful."

"Yeah."

We were quiet. The spring air drifted in through the window and ruffled the newspaper on my desk.

"I'll see what we got on Deleon," Quirk said, "if anything."

"Maybe you should check out Lisa's background, a little."

"We have, a little," Quirk said.

"And?"

"Goes back a couple years," Quirk said, "without anything unusual— and then nothing. It's like she didn't exist prior to 1990."

"How hard did you look?"

"Hard enough. We lifted some prints from the house that are probably hers. We're waiting to hear."

"What about her references and stuff at the radio station?"

"Checked them," Quirk said. "They never heard of her."

"Previous employment, all that?"

"Fake."

"Academic credits when she entered Merrimack State?"

"None required. It's open enrollment, continuing education."

"Might explain the everything-started-the-night-we-met deal she had with Belson," I said.

"Might," Quirk said.

"Anybody named Vaughn crop up while you were looking?"

"Yeah, I saw that on the calendar pad," Quirk said. "Whoever he is, I haven't found him."

"You got anything on the shooting?"

"One of the neighbors is a nurse. Husband's a gastroenterologist at Brigham. She was coming home from Faulkner Hospital after work, says she saw a yellow van parked by the pond a little before the shooting. Said she noticed it because of how it was kind of ugly for the neighborhood."

"She didn't get a plate number."

" 'Course not. Doesn't know what kind of van or what year. Just an ugly yellow van."

"Anything on the bullets?"

"They were nine millimeter Remingtons, we found the brass."

"That narrows it down," I said.

"Yeah," Quirk said. "In Proctor they sell them in vending machines."

"You think it's connected to Lisa?"

"Yeah."

"Doesn't have to be," I said.

"That's right, what do you think it's connected to?"

"Lisa," I said. "Let me know when you get something on the prints."

"Sure," Quirk said.

The slim gray-haired woman with the young face came into the room and took away the dishes. There was a single silver streak in her hair. She was dressed in jeans and a pink sweatshirt. She neither looked at Lisa nor spoke. She was careful not to look at the glowing video monitors where the tapes ran their endless loops. As the woman left, Lisa could see past her into the hallway outside the door, where a man in a flowered shirt open over his undershirt leaned on the wall. She could see the butt of a handgun stuck into his belt, to the right of the buckle. The door closed. She heard the key turn. Then silence, except for the soft electronic hum of the monitors. She walked about the room. She went into the bathroom and looked at herself in the mirror. She was wearing a safari outfit today, like Deborah Kerr in King Solomon's Mines. He had chosen it, and she didn't argue. She had decided soon after she was captured that she wouldn't fight the small battles. He wanted her to dress up like the movies, it would do her no harm. She was waiting for the big battle. She would have only one chance and she didn't want to squander it. She couldn't do it yet because it would do her no good to hit him and flee when an armed guard stood outside the door. The less trouble she gave him, the more he might be careless. And maybe once the door would be unlocked. Maybe once there would be no armed guard. And if the door were always locked and the guard always there and the chance never materialized? . . . Frank would come, sooner or later, he'd show up. She knew that. And knowing something certain was a handhold on sanity. She smoothed her hair back from her forehead and looked at herself in the mirror. She looked like she always looked. It was probably a truth about tragedy, she thought, while the tragedy is going on people look pretty much the way they looked when it wasn't. She turned and walked back into the bedroom. The monitors were looping the tape of her kidnapping, herself lying bound on the floor in the back of his van. She paid them no attention. She was hardly aware of the monitors at all. They had become so much a part of her limited landscape that they were barely tangible.

Behind her she heard the key in the door lock, and then he came into the room.

"Chiquita," he said. "You look just as I'd hoped. Turn around, please. All the way around. Now walk toward me. Yes. It is just as I'd hoped."

He was wearing a loose-fitting white shirt, with big sleeves. The shirt was open at the neck and unbuttoned halfway to his waist. He wore tan rid-

ing breeches and high cordovan-colored riding boots. She tried to remember the movie poster he was modeling. Lives of a Bengal Lancer? Elephant Walk? *She couldn't remember. But she knew that he coordinated what he would wear with the way he dressed her. He would lay out her clothes before he left her the night before, if it was night. She never knew. When he came in the next day, if it was the next day, he would be costumed to match. His very own, anatomically correct mannequin, she thought as she modeled her outfit. He smiled at her and put out his arm, crooked, as if for a promenade.*

"Come, querida, I have a treat for you."

She remained unmoving, not sure what he wanted.

"Come, come," he said. "We will take a little walk. It is time the queen toured her realm."

She walked slowly to him, and put her hand on his arm lightly. And they turned and walked out the door.

Chapter 14

I took off my tool belt and hung it on a nail on one of the bare studs in the torn-out living room of the old farm house we were rehabbing in Concord, Mass., about three miles from the rude bridge that arched the flood. It was lunch time. Susan had gone out and bought us some smoked turkey sandwiches on homemade oatmeal bread at Sally Ann's Food Shop. Now she was back and we sat out at our picnic table on the snow-melt marshy grass in the yard and ate them, and drank Sally Ann's special decaf blend from large paper cups.

"I don't know why you kvetch so about decaffeinated coffee," Susan said. "I think it tastes perfectly fine."

Pearl the Wonder Dog hopped up onto the picnic table and stared at my sandwich from very close range. I broke off a piece and gave it to her. It disappeared at once and she resumed the stare.

"You lack credibility, Suze," I said. "You could live on air and kisses sweeter than wine."

Susan gave half her sandwich to Pearl.

"This is true," Susan said. "But I still can't tell the difference."

Pearl stared at my sandwich some more, her eyes shifting as I took a bite.

"You know, when I was a kid," I said, "neither my father nor my uncles would let the dog up on the dining room table. Not even Christmas."

"How old fashioned," Susan said.

It was one of the first warm days of the year, and the sun was very satisfying as it seeped through my tee shirt. I took one final bite of the sandwich and gave the rest to Pearl. It was big enough to be taken someplace, so Pearl jumped off the table and went into the house with it. Susan looked at me with something which, in a lesser woman, would have been a smirk.

"It's the gimlet eye," I said. "I get worn down."

"Anyone would," she said. "How is Frank?"

"I guess he's going to make it, but he's still in intensive, still full of hop and drifting in and out. And they still don't know when he'll walk."

"Are you making any progress finding Lisa St. Claire?"

"I've found an old boy friend," I said.

"Cherchez l'homme," Susan said.

"Maybe. He's an Hispanic guy from Proctor named Luis Deleon. He might be the one on her answering machine that might have had an accent and said he'd stop by later. I played the tape for Lisa's friend Typhanie—with a *y* and a *ph*—and she couldn't say for sure, but it might be him. He's apparently the guy Lisa was with before Belson."

"And you think she might be with him?"

"I don't know. Awful lot of might-be's. But I don't have anyplace else to look, so I'll look there."

"I hope she's not with someone," Susan said.

"Yeah. But, in a sense, if she is, Belson will know she's not dead, and he'll know what he has to fight."

"The voice of experience."

"Disappearance is terrifying," I said. "Whether me or him is painful, but it's clear."

"And you've not spoken with Frank about this?"

"Mostly he doesn't know what day it is," I said. "But even if he did, what's to talk about?"

"One would assume if you were looking for a man's wife, you would want to talk with him about it if possible. If only to offer him emotional support."

"He won't want to talk about it," I said. "Except as a case."

"Maybe you should help him, when he's able."

"Some people," I said, and stopped and took a significant bite of the second sandwich, "even some very intelligent people, even now and then some very intelligent shrinks, sometimes think that not talking about things is a handicap. For the people who aren't talking about things, however, it is a way to control feelings so you won't be tripping over them while you're trying to do something useful. Containment is not limitation. It is an alternative to being controlled by your feelings."

Susan smiled.

"How artful," she said. "You're talking about men and women, but you don't specify."

"I don't think it's necessarily gender differentiated," I said. "Lot of women are critical of a lot of men on the issue, and a lot of men feel that women don't get it. But I hate to generalize. You, for instance, are very contained."

"And there are moments when you are not."

Pearl came loping back from the house toward my second sandwich. There was an accusatory look to her as she came, unless that was just projection on my part. I got another large bite in before she reached me.

"Like when?" I said around the bite.

"You know," Susan said. "I don't wish to speak of it in front of the baby."

"She has to know sometime," I said.

Pearl rested her chin on my knee and rolled her eyes up to look at me. I gave her the remainder of my sandwich.

"I think she knows everything she needs to know, now," Susan said. Pearl bolted down the remainder of my lunch and wagged her tail.

"You won't tell the guys, will you?" I said. "That the dog bullies me?"

"No," Susan said. "Or that you let me see your emotions from time to time."

"Whew!"

"Have you located this man Deleon?"

"No. I've talked to the cops and a priest. He's somewhere in Proctor. Monday, I'm going to talk to a guy named Freddie Santiago, who's sort of the mayor of Hispanic Proctor."

"Isn't that most of Proctor?"

"Yeah, nearly all."

"But he isn't the real mayor."

"He may be the real mayor. But the official mayor is a guy named Harrington."

"Is Hawk helping on this?"

"Hawk's in Burma," I said. "Right now, I need someone who speaks Spanish."

"Burma? What can Hawk be doing in Burma?"

"Better not to know," I said. "Gives us deniability."

Chapter 15

When he came into the coffee shop at the Park Plaza, Quirk looked like he always did, thick bodied, neat, clean shaven, fresh haircut, hands like a mason. Today he wore a blue suit and a blue-and-white striped shirt. He slid into a seat across from me and ordered some coffee.

"Deleon is dirty," he said.

"Not a surprise," I said. "How bad is it?"

"Pretty bad," Quirk said. "He's been arrested twice on assault, once on possession with intent . . . once for rape. He walked on both assault charges when the witnesses failed to appear. He walked on the rape charge when the victim recanted. He got a suspended sentence and three for the possession with intent."

"The wheels of justice grind exceeding slow," I said.

"Don't they?" Quirk said. "He is suspected of, but never charged with, several murders associated with the drug trade, and probably some homicides related to some kind of sporadic turf war going on up there between him and Freddie Santiago. Freddie's got them outnumbered, I'm told, and owns most of the city. But Deleon and his outfit are so mean and violent and plain fucking crazy that Freddie has never had the nads to go into San Juan Hill and dig them out."

I nodded. A waitress came over and poured coffee into Quirk's cup.

"Would you like a menu?" she said.

Quirk said, "No, you got a couple plain donuts?"

The waitress said that she had and went to get them.

"You got any history on him?" I said.

"More than you want to read," Quirk said. "Department of Ed's got core evaluations. DYS got counseling reports. There's a file in the Department of Employment and Training, the Probation Commission, Department of Social Services, Public Welfare, probably the Mass. Historical Commission. If there was a state service this kid used it."

"How old is he?"

"Twenty-six. Born in Puerto Rico, came here as a baby. His mother was a hooker, father unknown. Mother was a crack head, committed suicide ten years ago. No record of him finishing school. He was in an outreach program at Merrimack State for a while. Which is probably where he met Lisa. Started in 1990. Lisa was there then."

The waitress returned with the donuts. She refilled Quirk with real coffee and freshened up my decaf.

"Got a picture?" I said.

Quirk nodded and handed me a mug shot, full face and profile. The first thing I noticed was that women would think he was handsome and most men wouldn't. He had a thin face with big dark eyes, and a strong nose. His hair looked longish and he was probably twenty-one or -two in the mug shot. I read his stats on the back: 6'5", 200 pounds. We were in the same weight class, but he'd have reach on me.

"DYS counseling report says he shows signs of incipient paranoid schizophrenia and is deemed capable of sudden violent rages."

"Sounds like you," I said.

"Yeah, I'd probably have incipient paranoid schizophrenia, if I knew what it meant. You interested in the prints we lifted on Lisa?"

"Isn't that cute," I said. "Yes, Lieutenant, I am agog with interest."

"Nice of you to notice that I'm cute," Quirk said. "Prints belong to somebody named Angela Richard." He gave it the French pronunciation. "She was busted in LA in 1982 and again in '85 for soliciting."

"No mistakes?" I said.

"No, they sent us her pictures. It's Lisa."

"Jesus Christ," I said. "Belson know?"

"Not yet."

"You going to tell him?"

"No, you?"

"Not yet," I said.

Quirk picked up his second donut, leaned back in his chair and looked past me out the big plate glass window at Park Square, where the yellow cabs were queuing up near the hotel entrance. The doormen were opening their doors with a flourish and pocketing the tips deftly.

Quirk said to me, "You got some connections in LA, don't you?"

"Cop named Samuelson," I said. "LAPD."

Quirk nodded.

"You decide you want to bust that tenement up in Proctor, gimme a shout."

"Sure," I said.

Quirk finished his donut and left. I watched him as he walked past the picture window, a big, solid, tough guy, whose word you could trust. He swaggered a little, the way cops do, as he walked toward St. James Avenue.

Chapter 16

Susan and I were aboard American flight number 11 when it took off without incident at nine a.m. We ate breakfast on the plane and speculated between ourselves as to what it was. Then Susan put on her earphones to watch the movie. And I settled in to read the rest of my current book, *Streets of Laredo,* and worry about crashing. I worried less while we were flying along. They didn't usually fall suddenly from the sky.

"It's just a control issue," Susan said. "The drive to the airport is probably more dangerous."

"You think it's too early to start drinking?" I said.

"Well." Susan looked at her watch. "It's about seven a.m. in Los Angeles."

"Right," I said. "The movie any good?"

"Oh God, no," Susan said. "It's hideous."

"So how come you're watching it?"

"So I won't think about how high we are," she said.

"You're scared too."

"Of course I am," Susan said and smiled at me. "But I'm a girl."

Over Flagstaff, Susan took her earphones off and said, "Why was it, exactly, that we are going to Los Angeles?"

"To check into the Westwood Marquis and have sex," I said.

Susan nodded.

"Check in, *unpack,* and have sex," she said.

"Of course."

"Didn't you say there was something to do with Frank's wife?"

"Quirk ran down her fingerprints," I said. "LAPD arrested her for prostitution. Twice, 1982 and 1983. At that time her name was Angela Richard."

"My God, does Frank know this?"

"If he does, he's kept quiet about it," I said. "We haven't told him."

We were just above the San Gabriel Mountains now, so close that it seemed you could step out onto one of the peaks.

"And you want to see if you can get some information out here that will help you find her?"

"Yeah."

"How's that going to work?" Susan said.

"I don't know. Maybe it won't. I got no master plan, I feel my way along."

"Why should you be different?" Susan said.

We slid past the San Gabriels, drifted down over the San Fernando Valley, landed without crashing, got our rental car, and drove in from the airport on 405.

"Do we know how old Lisa is?" Susan said.

"Gave her age as nineteen in 1982," I said. "If she was telling the truth, makes her thirty-one."

"I could have done the math," Susan said, "in time."

"Yeah, but we're only here a few days," I said.

The Westwood Marquis is located just out of Westwood Village, across from UCLA Medical Center. It has two pools, a health club, and a spectacular brunch, and a lot of gardens. Our room was painted blue. It had a small sitting room, a bath, and a bedroom with a big bed and a bank of mirrored closet doors. Susan looked at them and looked at the bed.

"Are you going to peek?" she said.

"You bet your boots," I said.

"Pornographer," Susan said and began to unpack. To watch Susan unpack was to witness a process as elaborate and careful as a spider weaving a web. While she carefully unfolded and shook out and hung each item behind the mirrored doors, I took a shower and put on one of the terrycloth robes the hotel provided. It fit me like a hot dog casing on a knockwurst. Susan finished her unpacking, ran a bath, and went into the bathroom "to fluff up." I closed all the mirrored doors she had left open, and checked the angle of reflection. After a while Susan emerged with a white terrycloth robe clutched voluminously around her.

"First we'll have to agree that there'll be no peeking in the mirror," she said.

"Of course not," I said. My voice was rich with sincerity.

"Can you get your arms out of those bathrobe sleeves?" she said to me.

"Probably," I said.

"Well, why don't you?"

Later in the afternoon we lay quietly in the bed together, with Susan's head on my shoulder.

"What's the plan?" she said.

"I know a cop out here named Samuelson," I said. "Met him when I was out here with Candy Sloan a long time ago."

"I remember."

"I called him a couple of days ago. He said he'd dig up Angela Richard's file and I promised him lunch at Lucy's."

"And then?"

"And then we'll see," I said.

We were quiet for a time, listening to the faint hum of the air conditioner, watching the sunlight on the blue walls. Susan turned her head on my shoulder and looked straight at me from maybe six inches away. Amusement moved in her big eyes, and something else, a hint of depravity, or joy, or excitement, or all three, that I'd never quite been able to figure out.

"Did you peek?" Susan said.

"Absolutely not," I said.

"Are you lying?" she said.

"Absolutely am," I said.

They walked out into the corridor. The guard was there. Not the same one she'd seen earlier; they probably changed shifts frequently. The floor of the hallway was linoleum which had been painted with maroon deck paint so that it had once had a shiny gloss. But the linoleum had buckled and there were cracks spidering across the enameled surface, and the sheen was nearly gone. She felt almost dizzy at coming out of the room into the daylight. It was like the way she felt coming out of an early afternoon movie. She had not seen daylight since he'd brought her here. Before them a small-boned, black-haired young man with two long braids and a blue bandanna tied into a head band like Willie Nelson was backing down the corridor ahead of them, the video camera leveled, the tape whirring faintly. The corridor walls were half paneled with narrow grooved red oak boards that had been varnished once, and were now almost black with age and dirt. The walls above were white-painted plaster grown gray by the same process that had aged the oak wainscotting. "Downstairs, Lisa mia, your people are waiting to greet you."

My people, I don't have any goddamned people. Frank is my people. She kept her face composed. At least she didn't look as ridiculous in her safari outfit as she might have had he chosen to parade her about in her Moll Flanders outfit. They went down narrow stairs covered with frayed rubber mats on each step so you shouldn't slip. At the bottom was the kitchen, with a huge old yellow Glenwood gas range that stood on bowed black legs. The sink was soap stone, and two shabby-looking refrigerators stood side by side against the left-hand wall. One of them had the condenser equipment on top of it. A big table occupied the middle of the room. It was the kind that hotels use to set up banquet rooms. It had a splintery plywood top, and folding metal legs. There were some flowers in a coffee can in the middle of the table, and five or six assorted straight chairs set around the table. Five small children, three girls and two boys, were playing in diapers and little else, on the floor under the table. The slim woman in the pink sweatshirt who had brought Lisa's food was there, and a fat woman in a tight lavender sweatsuit. They were sitting at the table, minding the children, eating occasionally from a large open bag of Vincent potato chips that lay on its side on the table.

Luis said something to them in Spanish. They stared at her and nodded.

"Lisa," Luis said, "this is my cousin Evangelista, and my friend Chita."

"*Do you know that he has kidnapped me?*" Lisa said.

The two women looked at her without expression.

"*That is a bad word to use here, Lisa,*" Luis said. "*I have simply re-claimed what is mine. And, of course, they do not speak English.*"

Beyond the women at the table a door led into the backyard. Through it she could see small children, somewhat older than the babies in the kitchen, playing in the courtyard formed by the enclosing tenements. He walked with her to the door. She went volitionlessly, and stood silently beside him on the back step. There was a bent and rusty metal swing set on one side of the yard, and a pile of sand on the other. The grass had been worn away and the earth was bare and muddy from the rain. Each of the tenements had a back porch on each floor and en masse they rose like balconies in a de-crepit theater. On the first-floor back porch directly opposite her, seated among the pieces of wash hanging damp on the sagging clothesline, two young adolescent girls watched the children.

"*We use the courtyard for the children,*" he said. "*They are safe here.*"

Lucky them, Lisa thought.

Chapter 17

Lucy's El Adobe is a very ordinary-looking restaurant in Hollywood, right across from the Paramount Gate. When we got there Samuelson was already in a booth drinking coffee and looking at nothing and seeing everything. He was a rangy guy with a square face and very little hair. He wore tinted glasses and his moustache was trimmed shorter since I'd seen him last. He nodded when he saw me come in and stood when he saw Susan. I introduced them.

"You're the one he went home to," Samuelson said.

"I believe I am," Susan said.

"Can't say I blame him," Samuelson said.

Susan ordered a frozen margarita, with salt. I glanced at her and she smiled serenely. Samuelson had more coffee and I ordered decaf. Samuelson looked disgusted.

The waitress brought the drinks, took our food orders, and went away.

"You ever hear from Jill Joyce?" Samuelson said.

"No. Vincent del Rio still around?"

"Like death and taxes," Samuelson said. "I never figured how you didn't irritate him."

"Same way I didn't irritate you," I said.

"You did irritate me," Samuelson said. "But the consequences aren't so serious."

The waitress brought the food. Samuelson had a taco salad, I had chicken fajitas. Susan had the combination special: chile rellenos, enchiladas, a beef burrito, refried beans, cheese, sour cream, guacamole. I stared at her.

Susan looked at her plate and said, "Yum."

"You going to be able to handle all that, little lady?" I said.

"I think so," Susan said. She grinned at me. "But thanks for asking, Peekaboo Boy."

"Why you asking about del Rio?" Samuelson said.

"I need a favor from him."

Samuelson said, "Good luck," and handed me a manila envelope from the seat beside him.

"Angela Richard," he said. "Hollywood Vice busted her twice, 1982, 1983. Sheriff's department got her once in '85. When the Sheriff's department got her they sent her out to detox in Pomona."

"Pomona?" I said.

Samuelson nodded.

"Busted her pimp, too," he said.

"That's unusual," I said. "LAPD or the Sheriff's guys?"

"Sheriff," Samuelson said. "I guess he hassled them while they were collaring her, so they hauled him in too."

"What's his name?"

"Elwood Pontevecchio," Samuelson said. "How many wops you know with a name like Elwood?"

"Anybody named Vaughn involved?"

"Nothing in the record," Samuelson said.

"Elwood do time?" I said.

Samuelson smiled at me.

"Sure he did," Samuelson said. "And it don't rain in Indianapolis in the summer time."

"Just asking," I said.

"Un huh," Samuelson said. "It's just make-work, you know it and I know it, and anybody ever worked Vice knows it. Sweep 'em up, process 'em, let 'em out. Pleases the righteous, and keeps a bunch of Vice Squad guys from getting into trouble someplace else. Why you interested in the hooker?"

"She's missing," I said. "Somewhere along the line she stopped being a hooker, changed her name, came east, and married a cop I know."

"And you're following up on a couple solicitation collars ten, twelve years ago? Out here?"

"Tells you how much I've got so far, doesn't it?"

Samuelson shrugged.

"Gotta start somewhere," he said.

"I take a ride out to Pomona, they going to be friendly about answering questions?"

"I'll give them a call," Samuelson said.

He paused as if the gesture embarrassed him. Then he spoke to Susan.

"Cop's wife, you know? I don't know him, but a cop is a cop."

Susan smiled at him.

"Certainly wouldn't want to do a favor for him." She nodded at me. "Would you?"

Samuelson grinned back at her. Susan could get a smile from a hammerhead shark.

"Peekaboo Boy?" Samuelson said. "He's so slick he doesn't need any favors."

Susan looked at me and the glint was there that I could never quite specify.

"Oh, maybe he does," she said. "Now and then."

Chapter 18

Pomona is a thirty-mile ride east of LA, on route 10, along a corridor of low shopping malls and office parks with black glass windows and big air-conditioning units on the roof. I was alone. Susan had decided to sit by the pool at the hotel with a copy of a book by Alice Miller called *The Drama of the Gifted Child.* I didn't mind. I was used to being alone. In fact, I liked it, unless it was for too long and I started to miss her.

The place wasn't called Pomona Detox at all. Its real name was Pomona State Hospital for Alcohol and Drug Addiction. The director was a psychiatrist named Steven Ito, and he talked to me in his cluttered office overlooking the employees' parking lot.

"My name is Spenser," I said. "I'm a private detective from Boston and I'm trying to find a missing person named Lisa St. Claire, who was apparently treated here in the mid 1980s under the name Angela Richard."

"I got a call from LAPD about you," Ito said. "They asked me to cooperate."

He was a well set-up Japanese man, with short black hair and strong hands. He had on a white coat over a blue shirt and flowered tie.

"Popular on both coasts," I said.

"No doubt, deservedly," Ito said. "How can I help you?"

"Do you have a record of Angela Richard being here?"

"Yes," Ito said. "I had it pulled when I knew you were coming. She was in fact here in 1985."

"Drugs or alcohol?" I said.

"Alcohol," Ito said, "which is not to say that alcohol isn't a drug."

"Sure," I said. "So is caffeine. How long she stay?"

"Three months."

"She sober when she left?"

"She saw a social worker every day, attended all her meetings, and when she left us, yes, she was sober."

"May I see the file?" I said.

"No," Ito said.

"The social worker still here?"

"No. Mrs. Eaton was married to an Air Force officer, a bomber pilot, I think, over at March Field. He got transferred to Germany in 1990 and she went with him."

"You have an address for her when she was admitted?"

"Yes. I'll write it out for you, it's in Venice."

He wrote on a prescription pad, tore off the top sheet and handed it to me. I put the address in my shirt pocket.

"Did you know her?" I said.

"No. I didn't come here until 1987."

"Anyone that might have known her?"

"I doubt it. There is rapid staff turnover. And even those who have remained with us have no reason to remember her. We get a great many people through here."

"How many employees you have on staff?"

"One hundred and fifty-three," Ito said. "Three shifts."

"You got a company newsletter?"

Ito nodded. "Yes," he said. "I could put a notice in there asking if anyone remembered her. Do you have a card?"

I gave him the dignified one, where it says *Investigations* under my name and address. The one where I'm pictured shirtless with a knuckle knife in my teeth I save for the hoodlums. Ito put the card in his desk drawer and riffled through the file again.

"She would be what, about thirty-one now?" he said.

"Yes. She appears to have turned her life around before she disappeared."

"Social worker's report indicates that she was eager, Mrs. Eaton says 'desperate,' to improve herself. Might she have simply left her husband as a means of continuing her self-improvement?"

"Husband's a pretty good man," I said. "But yes, it's possible. On the other hand, he was shot and badly wounded a few days after she disappeared."

"Which you assume is not coincidence."

"It's a useful assumption," I said. "It gives me a theory to work on."

"Yes," Ito said. He paused as he riffled the file and looked at one entry for a moment.

"Here's something," he said, "that may help you. Miss Richard was seen by a Beverly Hills psychiatrist named Madeleine St. Claire."

"St. Claire?" I said.

"Yes. She's quite a prominent doctor in Los Angeles, and once a week she comes down here and works with our patients. Pro bono."

"It's the name Lisa took when she came east."

"As you say, coincidences are not useful."

"You have her address?"

"Yes."

He wrote on his prescription pad again.

"And I'll call her if you wish, and tell her you're coming."

He handed me the address. I folded it and put it beside the other one in my pocket.

"You have my card," I said. "Anybody remembers anything about Angela Richard, you'll get in touch."

"Certainly," Ito said.

We stood. He shook hands with me.

I said, "Thank you, Doctor."

"Will her husband recover?" Dr. Ito said.

"From being shot, they think so."

"It is possible," Ito said, "that she is drinking again, and it is related to her disappearance. That sort of thing happens."

"I know it does," I said. "And I hope it's not the explanation."

"What explanation do you hope for?" Ito said.

"I'm goddamned if I know, Doctor."

"Yes," he said. "That makes it difficult."

Chapter 19

The Venice address was now a motorcycle repair shop, and probably not even that for long. The building smelled of decay and dampness. The paint had weathered off, and the framing around the doors and windows was sagging badly.

I talked to the proprietor, a tall bony guy in a Harley logo tank top and black jeans. He had a gold tooth and a three-week beard and the name Lenny tattooed crudely along both forearms. He was smoking a joint when I arrived, but it didn't seem to have made him mellow. He looked at me like I might be a field rep from the Moral Majority. I smiled heartily.

"Lenny around?" I said.

"I'm Lenny."

"Honest to God?" I said. "Talk about coincidences."

"Whaddya want?" Lenny said.

"I'm looking for a woman used to live here," I said. "Angela Richard."

"Never heard of her."

"How about Lisa St. Claire?"

"Never heard of her."

"Someone named Vaughn?"

"Never heard of him."

"Anita Bryant?"

"Never heard of her."

"Sic transit gloria," I said.

"Huh?"

"How long this place been a bike shop?" I said.

"Whadda ya mean?"

I sighed. "Are these too hard for you, Lenny? You want to warm up with something easier?"

"Hey, Duke. Don't get bright with me. I'll run your ass right out of here."

"Not unless you're better than you look," I said.

Lenny reached over and picked up a ball peen hammer.

"How good's this look?" he said.

I opened my coat and showed him the gun. And gave him a big charming smile.

"You a cop?" Lenny said.

"How long since this place was a house?" I said.

Lenny shrugged. He kept the hammer in his hand, letting it rest against his right thigh.

"I took the place over last year. Guy owed me some dough. It was a bike shop then."

"You around here in 1985?" I said.

"No."

"Where were you in '85?"

"I was outta LA."

"How far out? Chino, maybe? Getting tattooed?"

"I done a little time at Chino," he said.

"And you're probably a better man for it," I said. "Who around here was here in '85?"

"I don't know nobody around here. People come and go, you know?"

"I've heard that," I said and left Lenny to ponder his ball peen hammer. Nobody else in the neighborhood knew anywhere near as much as Lenny and several of them weren't as nice. After a couple of hours I gave up and cruised back along Venice Boulevard. I went under the 405 and, as a gesture of defiance, drove back to Westwood on Sepulveda. It took longer, but an easy gesture is hardly a gesture at all.

Chapter 20

I met Madeleine St. Claire for lunch at The Grill on Dayton Way. The place was so in that the entrance was hard to find, around the corner, off Camden Drive. It was an oak-paneled place which claimed to be famous for its Cobb salad. I'd been there before and on principle had never ordered the Cobb salad. The room was full of people, mostly men, dressed in expensive casual, and talking about movie deals. A couple of them were recognizable television performers. Some of them were doubtless agents, being as we were right down the street from CAA. And some of them were probably real estate brokers from Ventura. I didn't see anyone else who looked like a gumshoe.

She had arrived before me, which was one way to tell she wasn't a producer, and was already seated at a table for two, drinking tea. She was a small, sixtyish woman with delicate bones and short hair the color of polished pewter. She had on a very expensive fawn-colored suit and big round glasses with deep blue rims. Her pearls were probably real, and she wore a very impressive engagement/wedding set on her left hand. Her complexion looked like she spent a lot of time out of doors. Her handshake was strong when I introduced myself.

"Please have a drink if you'd like," she said when I was seated. "I have patients this afternoon, so I must drink tea."

"Thanks," I said. "But if I have a drink with lunch a nap sets in almost immediately."

"Pity," she said. "How may I help you with Angela Richard?"

"I don't know, really," I said. "As I told you, she's missing."

"Do you fear foul play?"

"No reason to fear it or not fear it, except that her husband was shot from ambush and badly wounded a few days after she vanished."

"Do you have any reason to think she shot him?"

"I have no reason to think anything," I said. "That's my problem. I don't even have some nice hypothesis to work on. I thought maybe you could give me one."

"I doubt it," she said. "It has been a number of years. And, of course, the therapeutic exchange is confidential."

"I understand," I said. "Are you aware that she took your last name? Calls herself Lisa St. Claire."

Dr. St. Claire nodded a shrink nod that acknowledged what I'd said without indicating a reaction. I had an impulse to lie on the table and recall my childhood.

"You found her at the Pomona Detox Hospital."

"Yes. I work there once a week."

"Is she an alcoholic?"

"No. She was drinking far too much and living self-destructively. But she was not addicted to alcohol. She was able to control her drinking."

"So she could, when you knew her, have a drink, without having six more."

"When she left me she was able to use alcohol in moderation," Dr. St. Claire said.

"Given your knowledge of her, Doctor, is she likely to have shot her husband?"

"From ambush, you say?"

"Yes."

"No. I do not believe she would have shot him from ambush."

"But she could have shot him under other circumstances?"

"I don't know could or couldn't. I will say that Angela lived a very harsh life, in very difficult circumstances. She had fewer restraint mechanisms perhaps than some women might have, and she harbored a lot of rage."

"At whom?"

"At her father, at her boyfriend, at men in general."

"Lot of whores hate men," I said.

"And have reason to," Dr. St. Claire said with a smile.

The waiter arrived. Dr. St. Claire ordered the Cobb salad. I did not.

"Would she have left her husband without a word?" I said.

"I don't know. She is not the same woman she was when she was with me. She became almost totally caught up in her own rehabilitation. She never missed an appointment with me. She read every book she could about self-destructive behavior, alcohol dependency, sexual relationships. She was fairly indiscriminate about it, and I used to urge her to be selective. I'm not sure all that reading helped her."

Dr. St. Claire smiled.

"An odd side effect was that while she was uneducated in general, because of all her reading she developed a highly sophisticated vocabulary, so that at one moment she talks as if she were a drill instructor, and the next she is discussing problems of identity and cathexis, or using words like 'adroit' or 'manipulative.'"

"True of a lot of self-educated people," I said.

Dr. St. Claire nodded.

"Whether this is still the case, I don't know," Dr. St. Claire said. "Time passes, people grow."

"Or dwindle," I said.

"That too," she said. "But in truth I wouldn't really be able to answer your question if I had just finished with her this morning. Humans behave unpredictably."

"There's some evidence of a former boyfriend on the scene. Guy named Luis Deleon," I said.

Dr. St. Claire shook her head.

"The name means nothing to me," she said.

"He appears to be a bad man," I said. "Record of arrests for assault, rape, and dealing narcotics."

"That is the kind of man that would have attracted her," Dr. St. Claire said. "She often expressed the wish to see her father again. Her father was a drinker and a brawler, in trouble often with the police. When he left her mother he kidnapped her and kept her for several months on the run. He didn't want her. He just wanted her mother not to have her."

"Father knows best," I said.

"It is her pathology," Dr. St. Claire said. "Angela experienced love as cruelty and exploitation. Seeking love she returns to cruelty and exploitation. The boy she ran away with is an example."

"Do you know his name?"

"I can perhaps recall it. It was an odd name. Oddly juxtaposed."

"Elwood Pontevecchio?" I said.

"Yes, that's the name. Isn't it an odd one?"

"He became her pimp," I said.

"Yes, I know. We were able to get her to separate herself from him. Though it was a struggle."

"What can you tell me about him?"

"He was abusive, and he was concerned with her only as he could use her. He seemed to hold her in great contempt."

"Ever meet him?"

"No. I know him only through Angela's description."

"You know where he is now?"

"No."

"She married a dead honest, straight-ahead, older guy," I said. "Who's a cop. You have anything to say about that?"

"An encouraging sign, I should think. Someone who might protect her from her worst impulses, or from their consequences."

"You know her father's name?"

"Richard, I assume," Dr. St. Claire said.

"You think she would go looking for him?"

"I don't know. Perhaps the men she found were a sufficient substitute. Perhaps they weren't."

The waiter brought the food. Dr. St. Claire had some Cobb salad. I took a bite of my chicken sandwich and washed it down with a swallow of de-caffeinated coffee.

"Know anyone involved in her life named Vaughn?"

"No, I don't."

"Maybe she didn't want the cop's protection any more," I said.

"Or perhaps she needs it more than ever."

"Her husband can't provide it right now."

"Then perhaps you'll have to," Dr. St. Claire said. "You look very competent."

I sipped from my cup again.

"My strength," I said, "is as the strength of ten because my coffee is drug free."

Dr. St. Claire smiled at me.

"How very noble," she said.

He pointed up. The tenements had flat roofs, like most three-deckers. She could see a man with a rifle leaning against one of the chimneys. There were other people up there as well, moving about.

"We have gardens up there, dirt dug from the courtyard, carried up by the bucketful until there is enough to grow our food. We have tomatoes up there, and beans. We have peppers, squashes. We grow cilantro. I will show you someday, chiquita, but not now. It is too soon. People might be watching. They might see you."

The thought that someone might be watching sent a jagged shock of excitement through her. She felt it in her buttocks, in the palms of her hands, at the hinges of her jaw.

"Have you seen someone?" she said, trying to keep her voice flat.

"No, but we are careful. I do not want you snatched away from me again."

She stared up at the rooftop, the man with the rifle, the people growing beans, she looked at the children playing in the excavated mud of the enclosure, and at the rickety porches that hung from the backs of the sagging gray buildings. She listened to the faint whir of the video camera as the young man with the braids moved about them, taping everything, preserving the moments. It had begun to rain lightly again. It never seemed to reach the level of a downpour, but it was frequent and often steady and everything had a wetness about it. The whole building complex seemed damp. It smelled of mildew. I'm not some debutante, she thought. I've seen worse than this. I've done worse than this. I've been worse off than I am now. And I've gotten out of it. I'm tougher than the son of a bitch, and smarter, and I'm not crazy, and he is. I'm going to get out of this.

She believed what she said to herself, but she also knew she had to control her fear, and what she didn't know yet was if she could.

Chapter 21

I sat in my blue hotel room while Susan ran up and down the stairs at the UCLA Track Stadium, and looked up Pontevecchio in the phone book. I found Woody Pontevecchio under Pontevecchio Entertainment, no street address, and a phone number in Hollywood. Spenser, master detective. I dialed the number and got his answering machine.

"Hi it's Woody. I'm probably out putting something together. But I'll be back soon, so leave a message, baby, and we'll talk."

I said, "My name is Spenser. I have something that will interest you about Angela Richard. Call me at the Westwood Marquis Hotel."

Then I hung up. It had to be him. How many Pontevecchios could there be who were likely to call themselves Woody? I went and looked out the window. It was a clear bright day in Los Angeles. Clear enough to see the snow caps on the San Gabriel Mountains. Mostly the caps were smogged in, but today they looked as clean and crisp as new linen. In the distance between the mountains and me was a complicated, often angry seethe of people simmering beneath the Southern California casual they wore like makeup. It was that juxtaposition of how it used to be with how it had turned out that made LA so interesting and so sad a place, I thought.

Behind me the key scratched in the door latch. It would be Susan and it would take her a while. Susan had some sort of key and lock handicap. The key scratched again, and the knob twisted. I waited. I used to make the mis-

take of opening the door for her to save her the struggle, but it made her
mad. She wanted to conquer the handicap. In the time I'd known her she'd
made no progress. The key turned the wrong way, and I heard the deadbolt
snick into place. The knob turned futilely again. Then silence. I heard the
key slide out of the lock. I smiled. I knew she was starting over. I looked
back out the window. Below my window a formation of feral green parrots
swept past above the olive trees, heading for the botanical gardens that ran
up Hilgard Avenue alongside UCLA Medical Center. There was some
more lock activity behind me and then the door opened and Susan came in.

"I knew you could do it," I said.

"It's not nice to make fun of a lock-challenged person," Susan said.

"Forgive me," I said. "I'm trying to be supportive."

"Why do you suppose I have so much trouble with locks?"

"Probably relates to your lack of a penis," I said.

She had on black spandex tights and a lavender leotard top, which was
soaked dark with sweat. Her bare arms were strong and slender with a hint
of muscle definition. She had on a white headband to keep her hair out of
her eyes, and her face glistened with sweat. I thought she looked beautiful.
She said, "Oink," and walked across the room. She bent toward me from
the waist, so as not to drip on me, and gave me a small kiss on the mouth.

"I'm a sweatball," she said. "I've got to shower."

While she was showering, Woody Pontevecchio called me back.

"Who's this Angela Richard you mentioned?"

"You remember her," I said, "back around 1985."

There was a silence on the phone. I looked at the mountain peaks. In the
bathroom, I could hear the shower running.

"I don't know what you mean," Woody said finally.

"Of course not," I said. "I'd like to meet you somewhere and explain
myself."

Again there was a pause. Out the window I could see a helicopter rise
slowly from the UCLA helipad, cant in the odd way that helicopters have
over the pad, and then move off above the rooftops of Westwood Village.
Through the closed window, in the air-conditioned room, the sound of it
was distant and small.

"Sure," Woody said. "Come to my club. Sports Club LA, you know it?
On Sepulveda just south of Santa Monica Boulevard. Ask somebody on the
desk to find me. Everybody at the club knows Woody."

"Be there in half an hour," I said.

Chapter 22

Sports Club LA is about the size of Chicopee, Mass., but slicker. There was valet parking, a snack bar, a restaurant, a sports equipment shop, a unisex hair salon, a pool the size of Lake Congamond, a full-sized basketball court, handball courts, a weight-training room with pink equipment exclusively for women, two aerobics studios, a coed weight room big enough to train the World Wrestling Federation, a vast onslaught of Stairmasters, exercycles, gravitrons and treadmills and, swarming over the equipment, a kaleidoscope of tight buns barely contained by luminous spandex.

The cutie at the front desk said of course she knew Woody, and wasn't he a trip, and took me straight to where he was on the second floor, in the coed gym. I felt as if I were wading in a sea of pulchritude. Like a rhinoceros lumbering through a swarm of butterflies.

"Here's Woody," the cutie said.

Woody was sitting on a bench, at a chest press machine catching his breath. He had on rainbow-striped spandex shorts and a spaghetti strap black tank top. His thick blond hair was perfectly cut, brushed straight back and held in place by a folded black kerchief knotted into a sweat band. He was tanned so evenly that he must have worked on it very carefully. He was lean and muscular. His teeth were expensively capped. And he had a small diamond in his left ear lobe. We shook hands. Woody was wearing fingerless leather workout gloves.

"Lemme just do this third set," he said, "then we can chat."

He lay back on the bench and pressed up 150 pounds ten times, carefully exhaling on each press, doing the exercise slowly and correctly. When he was through he sat back up and checked himself covertly in the mirror while he patted his face with a small towel and wiped the bench off. Then he turned and smiled a big wide perfect smile, crinkling his eyes very slightly.

"So, Spense, what's the deal?"

"Your first name Elwood?" I said.

"Yeah, is that a kick? My old man wanted to be a WASP."

"I'm looking for a woman named Angela Richard," I said.

"I'm looking for any woman I can get," Woody grinned widely.

"She was a hooker once," I said. "You used to be her pimp."

"Excuse me?"

"You turned Angela Richard out," I said. "Ten, twelve years ago. She got busted for hooking. You got busted for living off the earnings. Sheriff's department grabbed you."

"You are tripping, dude. I'm a movie producer."

"Easy segue," I said.

"This is ridiculous, you never heard of me? I produced *Malibu Madness* last year. I did a two-hour, for-cable syndication, *Don Ho's Hawaii.* It's playing all over the country."

"And the country's better for it," I said. "Sometime after she got out of Pomona Detox, Angela Richard moved back to the Boston area, changed her name to Lisa St. Claire, and married a Boston cop named Frank Belson."

"Man, this is ragtime. I don't know anything about this broad."

"After they'd been married maybe six months, she disappeared. And I'm looking for her."

"You a cop?"

"Sure," I said. "If you're a movie producer. Tell me what you can about Angela."

We were speaking softly. Just a couple of workout buddies gassing, maybe talking a little deal, the project's yours, baby, you run with it, I'll take a little up front for a finder's fee. Woody stood up from the bench.

"I think this conversation is over, pal. I don't have time to talk hip hop with some wiseass I don't even know."

"Oh, okay, Woody," I said. "I'll talk to these other nice folks."

I turned toward a young woman with a tight body and rippled stomach who was doing dips on a gravitron.

"Did you know Woody used to be a pimp?" I said.

She looked at me blankly for a moment.

"Hey," Woody said. "Hey, hey, hey."

"Shame he went down hill from there," I said to the young woman. "Now he's a producer."

"I don't know him," the young woman said. "And I'm trying to get a workout here."

Woody took my arm and steered me toward the vestibule between the two aerobics studios, where sleek people cavorted frantically near the front of the class in front of instructors wearing microphones and urging them on. In the back rows of both studios the action was a little more sedate and nowhere near as graceful.

"Lemme tell ya, I don't appreciate you saying things like that about me to people. I'm here to tell you I don't appreciate it one little bit."

A well-known actress with big breasts and thin legs walked by in a candy-striped thong leotard and went into one of the aerobics classes. She got in the back row and jumped around clumsily without too much regard for what the instructor was doing up front.

"Elwood," I said. "You stop pretending you weren't a pimp, and I'll stop telling people you were."

"That's a damn ugly word," he said. "You know that. Pimp is a nasty word. And I'll tell you something, I'm getting damned tired of hearing you use it."

"You knew Angela Richard, did you not?"

"So why don't you buzz out of here right now before I maybe get kind of mad."

I could feel myself smiling. I tried not to. I didn't want to hurt Woody's feelings. But I couldn't help it. I raised my forefinger in a wait-a-minute gesture, walked back into the exercise area, took the pin out of the 150-pound slot and put it in the lowest spot on the stack. I didn't bother to see how much weight it was. Most machines went up to about 275. I took off my beautifully tailored black silk tweed jacket with the fine cognac windowpane plaid in it that I'd recently ordered from a catalog, and hung it carefully on a curl machine nearby. I adjusted my gun on my right hip so I wouldn't lie on it and got on the bench and took hold of the handles and pushed up the whole stack and let it down and did it nine more times. Breathing carefully, keeping form. Then I got up and readjusted my gun and put my coat back on and walked back out into the vestibule between the aerobic studios and gave Woody a big friendly smile.

"That doesn't mean anything," Woody said. "I've seen guys can do more than that."

"Sure," I said. "Me too. Let's talk about Angela Richard."

The young woman on the gravitron got off and walked toward the triceps machine. As she passed the bench press station, she checked the weight and glanced covertly at me, only a flick of a glance at the weight and at me, but it was enough. I knew she was mine.

"I came out here with her," Woody said. "We were in high school together and we took off in the middle of senior year in my uncle's car and came to LA."

"What high school?"

"Haverhill High."

"Haverhill, Mass.?" I said.

"Yeah."

"By golly," I said. "Isn't it a small world, Elwood. You and she going to break into pictures?"

"Yeah." He shrugged. "We were kids. Angela was a real knockout, we figured she'd make it easy and I could manage her. You know? Even then I was a guy could put things together."

"So you lived for a while out in Venice."

Woody looked a little surprised.

"Yeah, and we weren't getting anywhere in legit films at first, so we did some adult films."

"Porn," I said.

"Yeah. Sixteen millimeter stuff, and then we came up with a really clever gig, for Angela to be a strip tease disc jockey."

"You thought that up, Elwood?"

"Yeah. I don't think anyone else is doing it. And we did that for a while all over, conventions, stag parties, that kind of thing. But there's so much competition in the market especially with video, you know? Videocassettes, home movies on video, and half the broads in LA willing to take their clothes off for nothing anyway. So we did a little hooking."

"You and Angela."

"Yeah, of course, who else we talking about? I put it together, she did the johns. We did pretty good till she got busted. She wouldn'ta got busted either, she wasn't drunk. I told her look out for the Vice Guys under cover. I could spot one two blocks away. But she's so drunk she drifted away from me one day and props one. By the time I get there she's in cuffs and yelling at the cop. I told her fifty times, you get busted, shut up, go downtown. Sit in the tank an hour. And I'll bail you out. But she's in the damned wrapper and she's yelling at the cops and I try to get her quieted down and the damned cops up and bust my ass. Put the arm on me. Sheriff's deputies. Those guys are the worst. City guys you can talk to, but the county guys, man-oh-man."

Woody shook his head. He looked at the clock above the second-floor balcony where the aerobic machines stood row upon cardiovascular row, ringing the exercise floor below. It was 5:05.

"I need a drink. You want a drink, man?"

"Sure," I said. "Replenish those electrolytes."

We went to the first floor and across the lobby and into the bar at the far end. The bartender was a neat, compact black man with a black and gold paisley vest over a white shirt.

He said, " 'Shappening, Woody?"

Woody said, "Hey, Jack. Gimme an Absolut on the rocks with a twist."

I ordered a beer. Now that he had given in, Woody seemed to be caught up in his own story and was pitching it to me.

"They held her overnight and took her out to Pomona in the morning. I tried to get her out, but they told me she didn't want to get out and . . ."

He spread his hands.

"I never saw her again. Too bad. I miss her, nice babe. Excellent look, you know."

He sipped his vodka.

"Oh-baby-oh-baby," he said. "The first one hits the spot, doesn't it, Spense?"

"Oh-baby," I said. "Why'd you run away?"

"Run away?"

"Yeah, during your senior year at Haverhill High? Why'd you and Angela run away?"

"Haverhill was a drag, you know. I was looking for some action."

"How about Angela?"

"Trouble at home," Woody said.

"You know where her parents are?"

"No."

"Brothers, sisters, cousins?"

"No."

"Know anybody named Vaughn?"

"I know a lot of people. First name or last?"

"I don't know."

"Don't mean shit to me," he said. "Singer named Jimmie Vaughn, Stevie Ray's brother . . ."

I nodded.

"Not him," I said. "Got any idea where she might have gone, or why?"

"Angela and I traveled together, Duke, a little grass, a little wine, maybe some poontang."

"What else is there?" I said.

Woody shrugged.

"Give her credit, though, she helped me get rolling out here."

He swallowed the rest of his vodka.

"And, let me tell you, Spense, I'm rollin' on the river out here now, rolling on the river."

I put out my hand. Woody took it. My hand was much bigger than his. I squeezed it. Woody tried not to show it, but I knew he was uncomfortable.

"I'm going now," I said. "I hope I don't have to talk with you again . . ."

I tightened my grip a little more, Woody tried to pull his hand away and couldn't.

"But if I do," I said, "and you call me Spense again, I will kick your ass around Westwood like a beach ball. Capeesh?"

Woody nodded.

"Good. Don't say another word."

I let him go and headed back to the hotel where I could wash my hands.

Chapter 23

Susan was standing in front of the full-length mirror in the hotel room wearing black-and-white striped silk underwear. She had a short black skirt with a long black jacket held up in front of her, and was standing on her toes to simulate high heels as she smoothed the skirt down over her thighs.

"L'Orangerie is dressy," she said.

"Yes."

She turned a little, watching how the jacket fell over the skirt, and then went back to the closet and got a pale gray pants suit and took it to the mirror.

"When we get to the restaurant," I said, "won't it be hard to eat holding your clothes in front of you like that?"

Susan's powers of concentration could set driftwood on fire. She ignored me, and in fact, may not even have heard me.

I got out my address book and thumbed through it and found a number in Los Angeles that I hadn't used in four years. I dialed it.

A voice said, "Hello?"

I said, "Bobby Horse?"

"Who's calling?"

"Your hero, Spenser, from Boston."

Bobby Horse said, "What the fuck do you want?"

"The usual adulation," I said.

"And?"

"And to talk to Mr. del Rio."

"Hold on," Bobby Horse said.

In a moment del Rio came on the line.

"Spenser?" he said. He always said my name as if it amused him.

"I need a favor," I said.

"I'll bet you do," del Rio said. "Why should I do you a favor?"

"We were okay on the Jill Joyce thing five years ago."

"Sí."

Del Rio did a movie Mexican accent when it pleased him to, though he spoke English without any accent at all. Hawk did some of the same thing. Amos and Andy one minute, Alistair Cooke the next.

"I'm looking for a guy's wife. Anglo woman. She might have disappeared into an Hispanic ghetto in a city north of Boston called Proctor. She might be with a bad guy."

"Sí."

"I need somebody speaks Spanish, doesn't mind bad guys."

"And I'm supposed to yell 'Ceesco, le's ride'?"

"Not you," I said. "I want to borrow Chollo."

"Ahhhh!"

We were both quiet for a moment.

"Why should Chollo do that?"

"Because you'll tell him to."

"Even I don't tell Chollo to do things, Señor."

Again del Rio paused.

"But I can ask him."

"Do that," I said.

There was silence on the line for a while.

Del Rio came back on the line.

"Chollo says he's never been to Boston and would like to see it."

"Like that?" I said.

"Sí. Have you seen Jill Joyce?"

"No," I said. "How is your daughter?"

"Amanda is at the Sorbonne," del Rio said. "She speaks fluent French."

"I'm in LA now, when do I look for Chollo?"

"He needs to finish up his current project. When are you going back to Boston?"

"Tomorrow. When will Chollo show up?"

"Soon," del Rio said.

"Does he know where to find me?"

"He'll find you."

"Thank you."

"Adiós, amigo," del Rio said and hung up.

Susan had on panty hose by now, and a pair of high-heeled shoes, and a honey-colored silk blouse. She was holding up a caramel-colored skirt and jacket in front of the mirror and looking at it approvingly.

"Remember before panty hose?" I said.

Susan turned a little to one side and looked at the caramel-colored suit from that angle.

"Garter belt and stockings," I said. "That was the look."

Susan nodded to herself and hung the jacket on the back of a chair. She scuffed off her heels and stepped into the skirt. Then she stepped back into her heels and put on the jacket.

"Everything new isn't necessarily better," I said.

Susan shook her head, took off the jacket, took off the honey-colored blouse, put on a gold necklace with some kind of amber stones in it, put the jacket back on, buttoned it, looked in the mirror, patted her hair a little, and turned toward me.

"Okay," she said. "I'm ready to go."

"So quick?" I said.

L'Orangerie had a bouquet of flowers in the center of the room that was about the size of a sequoia. Susan and I had roast chicken and a bottle of Graves.

"So has the trip been successful?" Susan asked me.

"All trips are successful when we go on them together," I said.

"Yes, they are," Susan said and gave me her heartstopping smile. "And did you learn anything that will help you find Lisa?"

"I gathered a lot of information," I said.

"Useful information?"

I shrugged.

"Don't know. You can pretty well guarantee that most of it won't be useful. This case, any case. But you can't usually know it beforehand. I just trawl up everything I can find, see how it works."

Susan carefully cut the skin off her chicken.

"Aren't you the babe that ate more Mexican food the other day than Pancho Villa?" I said.

"This isn't Mexican food," she said.

"Oh," I said. "Of course."

W e cannot spend the rest of our lives together without sex, Angel," he said.

It was the first time he'd brought it up directly. She felt her chest tighten and the sharp jab of anxiety in her stomach.

"We cannot spend the rest of our lives together, period!" she said.

She was wearing a plaid shirt and a buckskin skirt and cowboy boots and feeling like a chorus dancer in Oklahoma.

"We have had sex many times."

"I liked to think of it as making love, Luis."

"And you do not wish to make love anymore?"

"I do not love you, Luis. Remember? I don't love you."

"Love does not alter when it alteration finds," he said.

My God, she thought. He must have been preparing for this discussion. He must have looked that up in some quotation manual. She knew it was a line from some famous writer, but she didn't know which one.

"It should," she said. "If you change, your love changes."

"And you have changed?"

"Yes."

"I have not," he said.

He stood over her in black western clothes. She never remembered how tall he was. His childishness, his odd, sadistic vulnerability made him seem smaller to her than he was.

"I cannot, Luis."

"You cannot? Perhaps you will have to."

She shook her head stubbornly, knowing the futility of saying no in her situation but insisting on it, grimly, doggedly.

"I cannot, Luis."

Chapter 24

The morning after Susan and I came back from LA, I drove up to Haverhill, on a bright and charming spring Tuesday, to look for Angela Richard's parents.

I bought some decaf and two Dunkin Donuts. I thought you got more if you bought the Dunkins because of the little handles. The donuts made the decaf taste more like coffee and the weather made me feel good. Thinking about the trip to LA with Susan made me feel good, too. I'd found out some things and we'd had a good time. The things I'd found out didn't seem to be getting me any closer to finding Lisa St. Claire/Angela Richard. But I had learned when I was still a cop that if you kept finding things out, eventually you'd find out something useful, which was why I was heading for Haverhill. In my lifetime I'd had little occasion to go to Haverhill. I knew that it was a small city north of Boston on the Merrimack River, east of Proctor. I knew that John Greenleaf Whittier had been born there.

I parked out front of the public library and went in and got hold of the local phone book. There were five Richards listed. Four of them were men. One was simply listed as M. Richard, which usually meant a female. I left the library and got in my car and got out my street map book and did what I do. Three were nobody home. One was a young couple with a ten-month-old baby. M. Richard was it.

I said, "Do you have a daughter named Angela?"

She paused and then said, "Why do you want to know?"

She was a tall, stylish woman in a belted cotton dress. She had short salt-and-pepper hair and a pair of gold-rimmed glasses around her neck on a blue cord.

"I'm a detective," I said. "She's been reported missing."

"I'm not surprised," M. Richard said. "She has been missing much of her life."

"May I come in?" I said.

"Do you have some identification?"

I showed her. A short pale woman in a blue denim shirtwaist appeared behind her. She looked at me with no hint of affection.

"Everything all right, Mimmi?"

M. Richard nodded without speaking while she looked at my license carefully.

Then she said, "He's here asking about Angela."

"That's ancient history, Bub," the pale woman said. She wore her short blonde hair in a tight permanent.

"That may be," I said. "But she's still missing. May I come in?"

I gave them my killer smile.

"We can't help you," the pale woman said.

So much for the killer smile.

"It's all right, Marty," M. Richard said.

She stepped aside.

"Come in, Mr. Spenser."

It was a big old house with dark woodwork and high ceilings. The oak floors gleamed. The shades throughout were half drawn. To my left was a living room with sheets over the furniture. To the right was some sort of sitting room with heavy furniture and a cold fireplace faced with dark tile. There was a long sloping lawn in front, which set the house back a ways from the street. The walls were thick and there was very little sound inside the house when she closed the door.

We went to the sitting room. Marty kept her eyes fixed on my every movement in case I decided to make a grab for the silverware.

M. Richard said, "Will you have coffee, Mr. Spenser? Or tea? Or a glass of water?"

"No thank you, Mrs. Richard. When is the last time you saw your daughter?"

"Nineteen eighty," she said. "The night before she ran off with the Pontevecchio boy."

Beside her Marty snorted.

"Little Miss Round Heels," Marty said.

"Have you been in touch with her at all during that time?"

M. Richard's mouth was very firm.

"No," she said, "I have not."

"How about her father?"

"Mimmi, you don't have to go through this," Marty said.

M. Richard smiled at her gently.

"I'm all right, Marty," she said. "Her father lives or lived in Brunswick, Maine."

"Address?" I said.

"None, merely an RFD number," she said. "He wrote me a letter some years ago. I did not reply. Vaughn ceased to be of any interest to me years before his death."

"Vaughn is his first name?"

"His middle name actually, but he used it. His full name is Lawrence Vaughn Richard."

"Tell me a little about Angela," I said.

"She was a recalcitrant, disobedient child," M. Richard said. "She and her father drove me nearly insane."

"Tell me about it."

"He was a drunk and a womanizer."

"A man," Marty mumbled on the couch beside her. I'd probably wasted the killer smile on Marty.

"And she was his daughter," M. Richard said. "The stress of them drove me to alcohol addiction."

"From which you've recovered?"

"The addiction is lifelong, but I no longer drink."

"AA?"

"Yes. It's where I met Marty."

"And how come you've not been in touch with your daughter in all this time?" I said.

"She has not been in touch with me."

"And if she were?"

"I would not respond."

I nodded. The walls of the sitting room were a dark maroon, and dark heavy drapes hung at each window. There was a dark, mostly maroon oriental rug on the floor. Somewhere, perhaps in the draped living room, I could hear a clock ticking.

"All of that is behind me," M. Richard said. "Husband, child, marriage, alcohol, pain. I am a different person now. I live a different life."

I looked at Marty. She looked back at me the way a hammer eyes a nail.

"Did you know your daughter was married?"

"No."

"You ever hear of anyone named Luis Deleon?" I said.

"I have not."

"Lisa St. Claire?"

"No."

"Frank Belson?"

"No."

"Your daughter is also a recovering alcoholic," I said.

"That is no longer a concern of mine."

"Mimmi has no interest in your world any longer," Marty said. "Why don't you just get up and go back to it?"

Marty was very tense, leaning forward slightly over her narrow thighs, as she sat on the couch next to M. Richard.

"I never realized it was mine," I said.

M. Richard rose gracefully to her feet. Her voice was calm.

"I'll show you to the door, Mr. Spenser. Sorry I couldn't be more helpful."

"I am too," I said and gave her my card. "If something helpful should occur, please let me know."

M. Richard put the card on the hall table without looking at it and opened the front door. I went out.

She said, "Goodbye," and closed the door.

As I walked down the walk toward my car parked at the bottom of the sloping lawn, a bluejay swooped down, clamped onto a worm and yanked it from the earth. He flew back up with it still dangling from its beak and headed for a big maple tree at the side of the house. I got in my car. Be a cold day in hell before I gave either one of them a look at my killer smile again.

"Vaughn," I said to the jay. "Son of a gun!"

Chapter 25

The drive to Brunswick took about two hours, and locating Vaughn Richard's address in the city directory at the Brunswick Public Library took me another forty-five minutes. Fortunately there was a donut shop in town near the college and I was able to restore myself before I went out the back road, south toward Freeport, and found Richard's RFD box, with a pheasant painted on it along the left-hand side of the road. I turned off and drove down a two-rut driveway that ran through a stand of white pines and birch trees. The driveway turned past an unpainted garage with an old Dodge truck in it, and stopped in front of a small weathered shingle house on a hillside that looked out over Casco Bay. I got out of the car. A couple of long-boned hunting dogs, sprawled in the sun on the deck facing the ocean, shook themselves awake and barked. A tall guy with a long body and short legs came out of the house and squinted at me in the near noonday sun. He had shoulder-length gray hair, and a week's growth of white stubble. His white vee neck tee shirt stretched kind of tight over his stomach and his wrinkled khaki pants hung low on his hips, below his belly.

"Vaughn Richard?" I said.

"Yeah?"

I walked toward him. The dogs continued to bark, but they were merely doing their job. There wasn't much menace in it.

"My name's Spenser," I said. "I'm looking for a woman named Angela Richard."

The dogs circled around and began to sniff at me. I scratched one of them behind the ear, and the other stuck his head in to get scratched too.

"Why?" Vaughn said.

There was the smell of booze on his breath.

"She's missing. Her husband's worried about her."

"She got a husband?"

"Yeah."

"Shit, I didn't know that."

"Now you do," I said. "She your daughter?"

"You could say so."

"I could?"

"I mean, yeah, she's my daughter, but I ain't seen her in fifteen, twenty years. The old lady wouldn't let me near her."

"You wouldn't have any thoughts where she might be?"

"Hell no."

"You heard from her in the last few months?"

" 'Course not," Vaughn said. "She didn't want nothing to do with me."

"She told people she'd like to find you," I said. "She doodled your name on her calendar pad."

"My name?"

"Vaughn," I said.

"Yeah. That's me. Middle name, actually. You know? First name's Lawrence, but I never used it. She wrote it down on a pad?"

"Un huh."

"Why'd she say she wanted to see me?"

"Far as I know she didn't say. People she told assumed she wanted to come to some terms with her family, maybe put her childhood to rest."

The dogs got through sniffing and having fulfilled their contract went back to sprawling in the sun. There was a sliding door between the deck and the living room of the small house. I could see a quart bottle of vodka standing on the table, and beside it one of those jumbo plastic bottles of Mountain Dew. There were lobster pots piled against the house beyond the deck, and firewood in a wooden rack someone had cobbled together out of two-by-fours. At the foot of the sloping hill a skiff jostled on a short rope against a small jetty that looked no better built than the wood rack.

"She wanted to find me?" Vaughn said.

"So she said."

"What do you mean she disappeared?"

"Her husband came home one day and she wasn't there. No note, nothing. She was gone."

Vaughn frowned.

"You a cop?"

"Private," I said.

"Her husband hire you?"

"Yes.",

Vaughn had a prominent lower jaw and he shoved it out now so that he could chew on his upper lip with his lower teeth.

"You think she run away?"

"I don't know. Her purse is gone. And the clothes she was wearing. Nothing else. She didn't take any money out of the bank. There haven't been any ATM transactions. She hasn't used her credit cards."

"You think something bad might have happened?"

"I don't know what happened," I said.

"Shit, I wouldn't want nothing bad to happen to her."

"That's nice," I said.

Vaughn's eyes looked a little moist.

"Well, I wouldn't. I ain't seen her awhile. But shit, she is my little girl, you know. I had her with me for a while, 'fore the old lady got the cops on me, wouldn't let me keep her."

"And you been a regular busy beaver ever since trying to stay in touch," I said.

"I never knew where she was," he said. "I didn't know she wanted to see me."

His eyes were squinched up and he was actually crying. Tears and everything.

"I didn't know," he said.

I'd have been touched if I hadn't smelled his breath and seen the vodka on the table. I'd seen too many crying jags by too many drunks to be impressed with Vaughn. It was the kind of sorrow another vodka and Mountain Dew would fix right up. On the other hand, I saw no need to mention that his son-in-law had been shot.

"Ever hear of anyone named Luis Deleon?" I said.

Vaughn shook his head.

"Frank Belson?"

He shook his head again.

"Elwood Pontevecchio?"

"What kinda name is that?" Vaughn said.

"Ever hear of him?"

"No."

"Lisa St. Claire?"

"No.",

"Ever talk with Angela's mother?"

"Hell no."

"What do you do for a living up here?" I said.

"Lobster a little. Some firewood. Mow some hay. Unemployment. I make out."

"You have no idea where your daughter might be?"

"No."

He was talking all right now. His grief seemed to have subsided.

"What are the dogs' names?" I said.

"Buster and Scout. Buster's the one with the white on his face."

"They hunt?"

"Sure. Good hunters. Put some nice birds on the table in season."

I gave him my card.

"You hear anything, think of anything, get in touch with me. There may be a reward."

He nodded. I had made up the reward part, but I didn't want to depend too heavily on father love.

"You find her, you tell her where I am," he said. "Tell her I love her."

"Sure," I said. "I'll do that."

He was starting to tear up again. I got in my car and backed around and headed out his driveway. I could see him in the rearview mirror, standing on the deck watching me. Then he turned and went through the sliders back into his house. Vodka and Mountain Dew. Jesus!

Chapter 26

Chollo showed up at my office on Thursday morning. I told him what I was doing on the ride up to Proctor. If he found any of it interesting, he didn't say so. We got out of the car in front of Club del Aguadillano at 11:30 on a rainy April morning. There were three cars in the parking lot. Frost heaves had buckled the hot top years ago and weeds grew vigorously up through the cracks. The club itself was a cinder-block building, with a flat roof. The sign above the glass double doorway spelled out the name of the place in flowing pink neon script. On either side of the doorway someone had planted small evergreens in wooden tubs. The evergreens had never gotten big and now stood spindly and bare of needles in the spring rain. A blue Dumpster, overflowing with green garbage bags, stood at the corner. A railroad tie served as a step for short janitors. Beyond the club, the river ran a sullen gray, pocked by the rain and blotched with clusters of yellowish foam. From upstream, out of sight around the bend, came the unremitting sound of the falls. And from the club came the sound of salsa music.

Chollo stared at the club. He was slender and relaxed, with black hair to his shoulders, and a diamond earring. His thin dark face was more Indian than Spanish. He wore a black silk-finish raincoat, belted at the waist, the collar up.

"You fucking Yankees know how to do ugly," Chollo said. "I'll give you that."

"Hey," I said. "This is an Hispanic joint."

"It's Yankee Hispanic," Chollo said. "You could have more fun at the podiatrist."

"We're not here for fun," I said.

"That's good," Chollo said.

We went in. The room was brightly lighted, painted pink, and full of small tables and rickety chairs. The juke box was loud. There was a bar across the far end. Behind the bar was a huge bartender with thick forearms, a big belly, and a bald head. As he moved down the bar toward us, I could see the sawed-off baseball bat stuck in his belt slanting across the small of his back. He didn't look at me. He spoke to Chollo in Spanish.

"Tequila," Chollo said.

There were entwined snakes tattooed on the bartender's forearms. When he took the bottle of tequila off the shelf behind him and poured us two shots, the muscle movement in his forearms made the snakes move. He put the bottle back and bent over, rinsing some glasses in the sink beneath the bar. I took a sip. It was the worst stuff I ever drank. Especially in the forenoon. Chollo took a sip of the tequila. His face remained expressionless. He said something to the bartender. The bartender didn't bother to look up when he answered. Chollo translated.

"He says we do not have to drink it."

"What did you tell him?" I said.

"I told him his horse had kidney trouble," Chollo answered.

There were two men sitting with a woman, all of them Hispanic, at a table close to the bar. The rest of the bar was empty.

"I'd like to speak with Freddie Santiago," I said to the bartender.

He looked up briefly from his rinsing and looked at me without speaking. He had small eyes, made smaller by the puffiness around them. Some of the puffiness was age, and probably booze, some of it was scar tissue. Then he looked back at the sink. Two young Hispanic men in workclothes came in the room and walked straight to the bar. The bartender straightened and went down the bar to talk with them. There was a short conversation. They gave him cash. He took an envelope from under the bar and handed it to them. They left without looking at anyone. The bartender came back down the bar.

"Green cards?" I said pleasantly, being chatty.

The bartender rang the money into the cash register without paying any attention to me.

"Green cards," Chollo said.

A tall gray-haired guy in rimless glasses came out of the door at the end of the bar. He had on a three-piece blue suit. He looked at us for a while and then strolled down the bar. He spoke to Chollo in Spanish. Chollo nodded at me.

"You're looking to speak to Freddie?" the gray-haired man said.

"Yes."

"Why?"

"I'm looking for an Anglo woman who might be with a guy named Luis Deleon in Proctor."

"So?"

"A cop and a priest both told me that Freddie Santiago was the Man in Proctor."

"True."

"I want his help."

"And what does Freddie get?"

I shrugged.

"I'll discuss it with Freddie," I said.

The gray-haired man looked over at Chollo again. Chollo was leaning on the bar, watching the interaction of the two men with the woman at the table near us. He looked like he was having trouble staying awake. The gray-haired man nodded to himself and turned without saying anything else and went back through the door at the end of the bar.

We waited. The two shots of what might have been tequila sat in their glasses on the bar. We were brave, but we weren't suicidal. At the table near us the woman stood and went toward the ladies' room. The two men leaned forward and talked animatedly, their heads close together while she was gone.

A group of eight teenaged boys came in. They were Anglo and all of them underaged. Two of them wore green and gold Merrimack State warmup jackets. One of them, a heavy kid, strong and fat, who probably played football, yelled to the bartender.

"Hey Dolly, beer, huh? All around."

The bartender began popping the caps off brown beer bottles and placing them on the bar. No glasses. The kids came over to get them. The bottles had no labels on them.

"Ten dollars," the bartender said.

"Why don't we run a tab, Dolly? You don't trust us?"

"Ten dollars."

The fat kid grinned and put a ten-dollar bill on the bar.

"All the time we come here, Dolly. All the fucking good times, and you don't trust us."

Dolly took the ten-spot off the bar and rang it into the cash register and leaned against the back of the bar looking impassively at the kid.

"Laugh a minute, Dolly," the kid said and turned and swaggered back to his table.

Toughest kid on the football team, probably. It would have taken Dolly maybe fifteen seconds to put him in the hospital. The gray-haired man appeared at the doorway at the end of the bar. He said something to Dolly, who came down the bar to us.

"There," he said and gestured with his head toward the doorway.

Through the doorway was a big office, wainscotted in dark oak, the walls painted forest green. Along the back wall was a dark oak bookcase lined with hardcover books. I could see the complete works of Booth Tarkington and Mark Twain among others. There were some minions in the room, probably bodyguards, but the central figure was the middle-sized guy who sat behind a big Victorian library table, his hands folded quietly before him on the green leather table top. He was a trim man in a charcoal-gray suit, a white shirt, and a silver silk tie. There was a silvery silk handkerchief in his display pocket. His clothes fit him well. His nails were manicured. His dark face was leathery and pitted as if from a childhood illness. His nose was prominent. There were deep grooves running from the nostrils to the corners of his mouth. He nodded at us when we came in.

The gray-haired man said something in Spanish.

Chollo translated for me. "They are both wearing weapons, Chief."

"I understand the word 'Jefe,'" I said.

"Hell," Chollo said. "What do you need me for?"

"Let them keep the guns," Santiago said. He was looking at Chollo.

He spoke to Chollo in Spanish.

Chollo translated, "Who are you?" and answered in Spanish.

Santiago nodded.

"It will save us time," he said, "if we all speak English. You are Mexican, I can tell by the accent."

"Sí," Chollo said. "East LA."

"Had you been from around here," Santiago said, "I would have known you."

He looked at me without moving his head.

"And you?"

"Name is Spenser," I said. "I'm looking for a woman named Lisa St. Claire. She's missing. I heard she might be in Proctor with a guy named Luis Deleon."

"And you wish my help?"

"Yeah."

Besides Santiago and the guy with the gray hair, there were three other Hispanic men leaning on various walls of the room looking deadly and scornful, like a bunch of extras in a George Raft movie. In fact, the whole place had a kind of theatrical quality, as if it had been designed specifically as a dangerous gangster office. Freddie Santiago didn't take himself lightly.

"Why do you think she is with Deleon?"

"He is apparently her former boyfriend. There is a message on her answering machine the day she disappeared from a man who might have an Hispanic accent. He says he'll stop by."

"That's all?"

"They say the romance was a hot one."

"That's all?"

"That's all."

"You think that's enough reason to come poking your Anglo nose into my city?"

"It's more reason than I've got to poke it anywhere else."

Santiago smiled briefly.

"What will you do if you find her?" he said.

"That'll depend on her circumstances. First I'll find her."

"And her husband? Where is he?"

"Somebody shot him."

"Dead?"

"Almost."

"And this young man?" Santiago nodded at Chollo.

"My translator."

"And valet, perhaps? Does he lick your Anglo boots clean as well?"

Neither Chollo's voice, nor his face, showed any expression.

"You should be careful, Señor, of your mouth," he said gently.

Santiago said, "Julio, throw the Chicano out."

One of the background thugs heaved himself languidly off the wall and walked toward Chollo. He was maybe four inches taller and thirty pounds heavier. He had the bored look that thugs work so hard on. He put a hand on Chollo's arm. Chollo's hands moved so fast I couldn't quite tell what he did, but Julio was on the floor gasping for air and clutching at his throat, and there was a 9mm automatic in Chollo's hand.

"Mistake, Jefe, to let me keep my gun. You think because there are five of you and two of us . . ."

"Baptiste," Santiago said. "You and Tomás take Julio out until he stops choking."

The other two loungers came forward, watching Chollo out of the corner of their eyes, and got Julio on his feet and helped him from the room. Chollo didn't put the gun away, but he let the gun hand drop to his side, the barrel pointing at the floor.

"You are quick to take offense," Santiago said.

"We will get along better if you remember that," Chollo said.

Santiago smiled.

"I try to get along as well as I can," he said. He looked back at me. "And you, Spenser, are you also quick to take offense?"

"Not me," I said. "I am a pussy cat."

"That may be," Santiago said, "though you do not look like a pussy cat."

I smiled like I had a mouthful of canary and let it pass.

"I will think about your situation," Santiago said. "And, truthfully, will consider if there is anything there for me. If there is, I will be in touch."

I took my card from my shirt pocket and put it on Santiago's green leather table top.

"Call me," I said.

Santiago nodded.

"And you, my Mexican friend, are you moving here from Los Angeles?"

"Just here to visit my friend," Chollo said, "the pussy cat."

"And what do you do in Los Angeles? When you are there?"

"I work with a man named del Rio," Chollo said.

"Ahh!" Santiago said, and smiled as if this explained much.

Chollo smiled back, and as he was smiling the gun disappeared back under his coat.

"Ahh!" Chollo said.

He was on his feet now, pacing. She watched him struggle for calm, twirling the cigar slowly between his fingers. He had delicate hands, as she always imagined a surgeon's would be, and when he talked he used them expressively. He used everything expressively. His face was very alive, no matter how much he tried to keep it smooth. His eyes were big and they moved continuously, looking at everything, shifting endlessly. He had a big video camera in his hand, though he wasn't using it and appeared to have forgotten it. As he paced, he moved in and out of the small circle of light by the table.

"You cannot," he said. "You cannot keep saying these things to me, Angel. I love you too much. I cannot hear it."

"Then let me go," she said.

He had paced out of the light circle and she couldn't see him in the dark room. She had no idea what time of day it was and already was beginning to lose track of how long she'd been there.

"That is like asking me to die," he said.

He came back into the light, his narrow, beautiful, boyish face lit by the lamp on one side, still in darkness on the other. A half face, volatile and compelling . . . and crazy, she thought.

"Keeping me here is asking *me* to die," she said.

"To be with me, to live in wealth and excitement forever with me, is to die? Do you know who I am? Do you remember? Do you know what I have become? I have money, more than you can imagine. I control everything here. You can have anything you want."

"I want to be free," she said.

"Of me?"

"Everything isn't about you, for crissake, Luis. I want to be free, period. I want to choose what I'll do, and where I'll go, and who I'll love. Can't you understand that?"

"I too will choose, and I choose you," he said. "What has happened to you, Angel? The Anglo princess that used to make love to me, shamelessly? Are you now tired of the foolish Latino boy? Have you now decided to be an Anglo again and marry a stiff Anglo man and wear white panties and go to church?"

She could feel how shallow her breathing was. "If I'm going to make love, Luis, I'm going to do it shamelessly, you know? There's nothing going on to be ashamed of."

"We will make love again," he said. He was back out of the lamp- light circle again and his voice came seemingly disembodied from the darkness.

"No," she said and her voice was steady, although her breath came more rapidly as she was saying it. "We won't. Maybe you can force me to fuck you, but we won't make love."

He was silent in the darkness. Then the bright camera light came on, and the camera began to whir. Behind the light she heard him say, "I have learned, chiquita, to take what I can get."

Chapter 27

Chollo and I were riding in the back-
seat of a silver Mercedes sedan through Proctor. Freddie Santiago sat in the
front seat and the gray-haired guy with the rimless glasses was driving.
There was a black Lincoln behind us, carrying five guys with guns, in case
someone tried to spray-paint Freddie's windshield. It was another raw
spring day, heavy with the threat of rain, which had not yet been delivered.
It was nearly noon, and the unemployed men stood in groups on street corners. Some were on the nod. Some simply stood, their hooded sweatshirts
too threadbare, their baseball jackets too thin, shoulders hunched ineffectu-
ally as if even the spring warmth were not enough to ease the chill of de-
spair. On one corner there was a fire in a trash barrel, and eight or ten men
and boys were around it. There was a quart bottle of something in a big
paper sack passing aimlessly among them.

"Probably sherry," said Freddie Santiago. "Package store house label.
Costs $2.99 a quart, gives you a pretty good bang for the buck."

"Tastes like kerosene," Chollo said.

"Sí. But taste is not the point," Santiago said. "Like most people here
they have much time and little money. Sherry helps pass the time."

"So does work," Chollo said.

"There is no work," Santiago said, "except perhaps your kind, my
Mexican friend. This was a fine bustling mill city once, a Yankee city. Did

you see the fine clock tower on City Hall? Lots of Canucks and Micks came
in to work the mills. Some Arabs, too. Then the Jews came in and organized
the mill workers, kicked up the prices, and the Yankees moved everything
out . . . south, where the workers weren't organized and the niggers would
work for half what they were paying up here."

Santiago paused and lit a cigarette with a gold lighter. He checked to
make sure no shred of tobacco had fallen on his white raincoat. Spring outside the car was in full flourish early this year, but the impact of it in Proctor
was slim. No flowers bloomed, no birds sang, none of nature's first green
came golden from the earth.

"So there's nothing to do here, and nobody to do it."

"A perfect opportunity," I said.

"Exactly," Santiago said. "So the spics move in. And now there's nothing to do and a lot of people to do it."

Santiago exhaled smoke through his nose and smiled at us. He was sitting half turned in the front seat, his left arm on the back of the seat. He
seemed pleased with his small history of Proctor.

"So now there are the leftover Micks, who run the police force, and us,
who run the city."

I looked out the car windows at the lackluster tenements covered with
graffiti.

"Not too well," I said.

"No, not well at all," Santiago said. "For we cannot get together. As
your Mexican associate can tell you, the concept of Hispanic is a gringo
concept. We are not Hispanic, or, as they say on his side of the country,
Latino. We are Dominican and Puerto Rican and Mexican. We are like your
Indians in the last century. We are tribal, we fight each other, when we
should unite against the Anglos."

"They weren't actually my Indians," I said.

Santiago turned forward in the seat and rested his head against the back
of it and closed his eyes. He took a long drag on his cigarette and slowly let
the smoke out. The smoke hung in the car. Some other time, I thought, I'd
discuss the dangers of second-hand smoke with him. Right now I was being
quiet, waiting for him to get where he was going.

"I have worked very hard," Santiago said, "to unite these people in their
common interest."

The car turned right past a burned-out store front. There was no longer
any glass in the windows, and the front door hung ajar on one hinge. Leaves
and faded parts of newspapers had blown in and piled up against the back
walls. Diagonally down one of the dark side streets I saw the church where

I had talked with the priest who drank, and I realized that we were now twisting through the narrow streets of San Juan Hill. Behind us, the black Lincoln had come up close.

"But . . ." I said.

"But I am hindered by . . ." He paused. His head back, his eyes still closed, he seemed searching for words. Finally he shrugged and continued.

"Your man Luis Deleon, for instance, is such a person as hinders me."

I looked at Chollo. He nodded. I knew this was going somewhere and now we were nearly there.

"This is a feast, Señor Spenser," Santiago said, exaggerating the "Señor," in mockery of me or himself, I wasn't sure which.

"This is like the carcass of a great whale. There is enough for many sharks to feed. There is no need to fight. But Luis . . . he is young, he cares nothing for larger questions. He and his people say San Juan Hill is theirs."

Santiago shook his head sadly.

"As if one could own a slum, or would wish to," he said.

"Who owns the rest of the barrio?" I said.

Santiago turned back toward us. He smiled brilliantly.

"I do," he said. "But it is not such a slum, and I am a beneficent owner."

"Yeah," I said. "It looked great till we got in here."

"Give me time, Señor. I have not had enough time. I have spent much time putting down unrest and eliminating troublemakers."

"Except Deleon."

"Sí."

"How come he's still in business?" I said.

"He presents a challenge. He is himself a dangerous man." He looked at Chollo. "*Volatile?*"

"Same in English," Chollo said.

Santiago looked gratified.

"*Volatile,* and well armed. He has a large, well-armed following also. And where they live . . . it is a . . . how do I say . . . ?"

He looked at Chollo, making a looping gesture with his hand.

"*Laberinto?*" he said to Chollo.

"Maze," Chollo said.

"Exactly. It is a maze in there, tunnels connect houses, food stores, barricades. It is a nut that would cost a lot in the cracking."

"But it could be cracked," I said.

"By someone resourceful enough who found it worth the cost," Santiago said. "So far I have not."

"But I might," I said.

"Perhaps."

The car stopped at an intersection, then turned left. We passed an abandoned gas station, the pumps gone, the glass out, and the doors to the repair bay gone. Inside, a group of men gathered around the empty pit where the lift used to be. They were boisterous and excited. Above their excitement were the sounds of animals.

"Dog fight," Chollo said.

"Sí," Santiago said. "They put them in the pit and they bet."

"Fun," I said. "What do the dogs get out of it?"

"The winner lives," Santiago said.

We drove on. At the top of the small rise, at the intersection of two silent streets, we stopped. Across from us was a complex of three-storied, flat-roof tenements. Most of the windows were boarded up, though in some there were small openings as if someone had cut a square in the plywood. The clapboard siding on the buildings was probably painted gray once, but it was now peeled down to its weather-stained wood, warping in many places. The windowsills were beginning to warp and splinter as well.

"Those four buildings," Santiago said, "are Luis Deleon's castle."

The alleys between the buildings had been closed off with plywood so that the four buildings formed a kind of enclosed quadrangle. I wondered if Lisa was in there. If she were, it was a different living arrangement than she'd had in Jamaica Plain in the squeaky-clean condo with the Jenn-Air stove and the Jacuzzi.

"If he has the Anglo princess," Santiago said, "he has brought her here."

"But you don't know if he has her," I said.

"It pains me to say this. I know almost everything that happens in Proctor. But this I do not know."

"We need to know," I said. "And we need to know under what circumstances."

"Circumstances?"

"We need to know if she's there because she wants to be, or she's been kidnapped," I said.

"You think an Anglo woman would not wish to come here, with a Latin man?" Santiago said.

"They tell me she would have once," I said. "I need to know if she did now."

"Take more than love for me to move there," Chollo said.

Santiago shrugged. Beyond the derelict tenements, eastward toward the ocean there was a loud clap of thunder, and after it, the shimmer of lightning against a dark cloud that piled high above the roof tops. The rest of the day remained vernal.

"Vamanos!" Santiago said to the driver.

"Let's go," Chollo translated for me.

"I sort of got that one," I said. "Especially when we started right up."

Chollo said nothing. But his eyes were amused.

"What do you think?" Santiago said, facing back toward me.

"You figure if Deleon were out of the way, someone could unite all the Hispanic people into one effective block?"

"Yes," Santiago said. "I do."

"And whoever did that could control the city and the dead whale would be all his."

"Not a pretty way to say it, but this also is true."

"You got anybody in mind to play Toussaint L'Ouverture?"

"Of course it is me, Señor."

"So if I took Deleon out for you it would be a considerable favor."

"You believe you could?"

"If I have reason to."

"You are a confident man."

"I've been doing this kind of work for a long time," I said. "But I need to know what the situation is in there."

"And if I were able to tell you?"

"I wouldn't believe you."

"Be careful what you say to me," Santiago said.

"Nothing personal," I said. "But you know as well as I do that you could crack that place in an hour. You don't do it, because you are working really hard on being the hero of Hispanic Proctor, and you don't want to screw it by blowing up some of your own people. On the other hand, if you could find a few tough gringos to come in and do the job . . ." I shrugged my best impression of an eloquent Latin shrug.

"It would be cost effective," Santiago said.

"Yes it would, so if you tell me Lisa St. Claire is in there, and being held against her will, and I get her out and dump Deleon in the process, it comes out Jim Dandy for you. So why wouldn't you lie and tell me she is in there?"

"I told you I didn't know," Santiago said.

"Yeah," I said. "This helps your credibility. But a good hustle starts with letting the sucker win a little, doesn't it?"

Santiago smiled.

"So you won't trust me?"

We were out of San Juan Hill now, heading back south, toward the river. The streets were a little wider, but just as shabby. The black car behind us had dropped back a little.

"As one of our great leaders put it," I said, "trust but verify."

We were getting close to Club del Aguadillano. I had the rear window down a little and the sour chemical smell of the river drifted in. I could hear the sound of the falls in the distance. Santiago smiled pleasantly, without any warmth.

"And just how do you plan to . . . 'verify'?"

"Lemme get back to you on that," I said.

There was no natural day and night for her. She slept, she woke up. He was there, he was not there. This time he was not there, but there was a tray in the room, sliced tomato, a warm tortilla, and a thermos of coffee. Coffee. It must be morning. She sat on the side of the bed wearing pajamas supplied by him, slightly oversized, like the kind Doris Day wore in Pillow Talk. The video monitors were playing soundlessly. She had no idea how they turned on or off. She saw herself naked in the shower, and then walking naked from the shower straight into the camera. It played over and over again. There was always something playing on the video monitors. The shower scene, the scene of her bound in the back of the truck, the earlier scenes of herself and Luis at the beach. Scenes of her in her flapper costume, scenes of her asleep, all looped to play over and over, beacons of captivity in the darkened space. *I need a weapon.* On her breakfast tray was a spoon, fork, and butter knife. Nothing very deadly there. She'd read about people in jail making weapons out of sharpened spoons. She picked the spoon up and looked at it. She looked around the room. She had no idea how she would sharpen it. She poured some coffee and put in two spoonfuls of sugar. Outside the building she heard a rolling thunderclap. It excited her. It came from the world outside this room, away from the monitors. A world of movement and color, of sound and possibility; a world going sanely about its business, ducking into doorways, turning up coat collars, opening umbrellas as the rain began.

"You son of a bitch," she said aloud. "You can't keep me here."

She ignored the tomato and picked up the tortilla. She folded it twice and took a bite and began to walk around the room, chewing, looking for a weapon. The lamp was too puny looking. He was very strong, she knew. There was a floor lamp, but it had a skinny shaft and a wide, heavy base and was too unwieldy to be useful. She got down on her hands and knees and looked under the bed. There were bed slats holding up the box spring. They were a possibility, but they were rough, flat pine boards that were hard to swing or even hold. On her feet again, she finished the tortilla. The wardrobe was full of clothes on wire hangers. The theater flats that decorated the room were mostly plywood and canvas. Nothing she could pull off and use. Behind the flats, the walls they were concealing were crumbling plaster over lath. In many places, wide patches of the plaster had crumbled away entirely, exposing the scaly gray-white lath beneath it. Here and there, in the dimmish light from the lamp and the monitors, she could see vestigial scraps of old wallpaper, some several layers thick. Besides the roach powder, she could smell the tired mildew scent of an old building. She went into the bathroom. The back of the sink was bolted to the wall. The front rested on two chrome front legs. She felt one of them; they felt solid; she tried to wiggle it; nothing happened. She wished she knew something about how things were made. How would they attach those legs? She turned it. It gave a little. She turned again. Of course, they screwed on, that way they could level the sink. She carefully unscrewed it, and when it came away from the sink, she found that it was an iron pipe, encased in a chrome sleeve. She hefted the pipe. Yes! Then she carefully propped the chrome sleeve back up under the sink and took her iron pipe and hid it under her mattress.

"Now we'll see, you bastard," she said. But she said it soundlessly.

Chapter 28

Chollo and I sat in my car in the easy spring sunshine, drinking coffee and looking at Luis Deleon's redoubt. There was a bag of plain donuts on the seat between us.

"What you think you'll see?" Chollo said. He was slouched in my front seat, one foot propped against my dashboard. He always looked comfortable, even in uncomfortable positions.

"We got three possibilities," I said. "She's not in there at all. She's in there under duress, or she's in there not under duress. If she's in there and she's not under duress, I figure sooner or later she'll come out. Go for bread, buy a dress, go to a restaurant, walk the neighborhood, soak up the ambience."

"I been in jails got better ambience," Chollo said. "And if she is under duress—man I love the way you gringos talk—she won't come out."

"Right."

Chollo drank some coffee and rummaged in the bag for another donut.

"And if she's not in there at all, she won't come out."

"Right."

"So we see her, we'll know something."

"And if we don't, after a while, we'll have narrowed the possibilities from three to two."

"So how long you figure we'll sit here?"

I shrugged. Chollo found his donut and took a bite.

"How come it takes you all that time to find the right donut?" I said. "They're all the same."

"No two donuts are alike," Chollo said. "You had Indio blood you'd understand."

We looked at the house. A tall guy with a Pancho Villa moustache wearing a faded tan windbreaker and a San Antonio Spurs cap on backward leaned in the doorway. Chollo put his empty coffee cup on the floor and opened his door.

"I'm going to reconnoiter," he said.

"Yeah," I said. "Use that Indio blood, look for a sign."

Chollo got out of the car, closed the door, put his hands in his pockets, and strolled toward the tenement compound. I sat and worked on the coffee. Decaffeinated, with cream and sugar. If you drank some and then took a bite of donut, it wasn't so bad. In a while someone came to the door of the house and replaced the guy with the Pancho Villa moustache. The new guard was a fat young guy with a shaved head and an earring I could see from across the street. He was wearing unlaced high top black basketball shoes and a hooded red sweatshirt with the hood casually hanging to highlight the earring, and baggy pants with an extreme peg and the crotch at about knee low. The sweatshirt gapped over his belly and I could see the handle of an automatic pistol showing above his belt. As they changed places both guards looked over at my car. I didn't mind. If I stirred up interest maybe something would happen. Anything would be progress. Nothing happened.

I ate another donut. Susan had explained to me that they were not healthful, and while I was in favor of healthful, rice cakes and coffee didn't do it on a stakeout. Susan had explained to me that it didn't have to be rice cakes or donuts. Why not bring along a nice lettuce, tomato, and bean sprout sandwich? I told her if Chollo reached into the bag for a donut and found a bean sprout he would shoot me, and she'd have only herself to blame for her sexual deprivation. She smiled at me sadly and began to talk to Pearl.

The door opened and Chollo got back in. He reached into the backseat for the big thermos and poured himself some coffee.

"This is the real stuff, right," he said. "In the tan thermos?"

"Yeah," I said. I tried not to sound sullen. The decaf in the blue thermos was very satisfying.

"Place is a quadrangle, four tenements, all of them three stories, all of them connected by walkways from the third-floor back porches. The alleys between are walled up with plywood, and there's sandbags behind the plywood. There's some sort of wire fencing around the roof. It looks like they're growing plants up there. The windows are boarded up, with gun ports in them. There's a guard on one of the back porches, can see the whole interior of the quadrangle. There's at least one guy on the roof."

He sipped some coffee and made too much of how good it tasted.

Then he said, "I can hear kids in the yard in the center of the quadrangle. I could smell cooking."

"So it's not just pistoleros," I said.

"No."

"Doesn't make it easier," I said.

Chollo shrugged. We sat and looked at the tenement complex. Every hour, the guard at the front door changed. Each time, the new guard and the old one stared at the car for a time.

"Sooner or later," I said, "they are going to have to come over and ask us what we're doing."

"Sure," Chollo said.

We looked at the tenements some more. We were out of donuts and the coffee was gone. In the front seat beside me Chollo was quiet, his eyes half closed, his hands folded in his lap. I imagined myself from some distant perspective sitting in the car in the spring in a destitute city with a Mexican shooter whose full name I didn't even know. I also didn't know if I was looking for a runaway wife, or a woman who'd been kidnapped. Of course it could be neither. She could have been murdered, or died accidentally, or suffered a sudden stroke of amnesia. She could be in the tenement in front of me wearing black lace and serving champagne in her slipper, or chained in the cellar. Or she could be on a slab in some small town morgue. Or she could be in Paris, or performing with the circus in Gillette, Wyoming. All I knew for sure was that she wasn't sitting in my car with me and Chollo eating donuts.

Across the street a tall, thick-bodied man with a pony tail and a dark moustache came out onto the porch and talked with the guard. They both looked at my car. Then the thick-bodied man started down the stairs with the guard.

"Here they come," I said. "Sooner."

Chollo didn't stir, though his eyes opened slightly.

"Want me to shoot them?" he said.

"Not today."

"We going to talk to them?"

I started the car.

"No," I said. "Maybe next time. This time we'll run and hide."

"Okay," Chollo said and his eyes slitted again.

I put the car in drive and we left the two men standing in the middle of the street looking after us.

Chapter 29

I was in an eighteenth-century historical reconstruction called Old Sturbridge Village with Pearl and Susan. We were getting ideas for rehabbing our Concord house. Or at least Susan and I were. Pearl's interest seemed focused on several geese on the mill pond near the covered bridge. She went into her I-am-a-hunting-dog crouch and began to stalk very slowly toward them, freezing after each step, her nose pointing, her tail steady, one foot off the ground in the classic stance.

"What do you think she'd do," Susan said, "if we let her off the leash?"

"She'd stalk closer and closer and then she'd dash in and grab one by the neck," I said. "And give it a vigorous shake to break the neck and when it was dead she'd tear open its belly and begin to feed on its intestines."

"The baby? That's barbaric."

"Blood lust," I said.

Susan bent over and gave Pearl a kiss on the snout. Pearl gave her a large lap. Susan put her hands over Pearl's ears.

"Don't listen to Daddy," Susan said.

We took Pearl to the car after a while so we could go into the houses and other displays. There was a sign which said any dogs brought into the buildings had to be carried. Pearl weighed seventy-two pounds, and tended to squirm.

"I could carry her," I said.

"Of course you could, sweet cakes, and you wouldn't even break a sweat. But she likes to sleep in the car."

"Oh, all right," I said.

It was a cool, pleasant weekday and there were busloads of children shepherded by too few adults, jostling through the still village lanes, and milling around waiting for the snack bar in the tavern to open. A guy in breeches and boots and a white shirt and a high, crowned, funny-looking straw hat was spreading manure in a ploughed pasture.

"You want me to get one of those hats?" I said. "I could wear it when we made love."

"Depends on where you were going to wear it," Susan said.

We went into a large white house with clapboard siding.

"This is the parsonage," a lady said to us. She was wearing a mobcap and an ankle-length dress and seemed to incarnate eighteenth-century farm life.

"If you lived here you'd be the parson of that church there on the hill," she said.

"That would be a mistake," I said.

"Pardon me?"

I smiled and shook my head.

"The parsons were stern men, but good men," the woman said.

Susan smiled at her and we went into the parlor and looked at the way the blue painted paneling was finished around the brick fireplace.

"You think all the parsons were stern?" I said.

"Of course," Susan said.

"And all of them were good men despite their sternness?"

"Absolutely."

"Did any of them get to sleep with a sexy Jewess?" I said.

"Nope."

"No wonder they were stern," I said.

We went down the back stairs into the kitchen. It had a massive brick fireplace with a granite lintel. There was a fire on the hearth and a huge black pot on a black wrought-iron arm was swung out over the heat. I smelled cooking. Another woman in a mobcap was putting bread into the beehive oven next to the fireplace. I remembered Frank Lloyd Wright's remark about the fireplace being the heart of a house. Susan and I stood quietly for a moment, feeling the past creep up behind us briefly, and then recede. I looked at my watch.

"Twelve-fifteen," I said. "Tavern's open."

"Yes," Susan said. "You've done very well. I know it's been open since eleven-thirty."

"Hey," I said. "I'm no slave to appetite."

"Umm," Susan said.

We went into the elegant old tavern with its polished wood floors and its colonial colors, and paintings of stern but good men on the walls. We sat at a trestle table, as far as we could get from the children's tour groups, and ordered. Our waitress had on the implacable mobcap and long dress, adorned with a white apron.

"Might I have a mug of nut brown ale?" I said.

"We got Heineken, Michelob, Sam Adams, Miller Lite, Budweiser, and Rolling Rock."

I had a Rolling Rock, Susan had a glass of iced tea.

"How's Frank?" Susan said.

"He's awake more of the time now," I said. "But he has no memory of being shot, and still no movement in his legs."

"Does he know about his wife being a prostitute?"

"No."

"Does he know anything?"

"He knows that Quirk and I are working on it."

"What about the ex-boyfriend?"

"He's a little hard to talk with," I said. "Being as he lives in what appears to be some sort of three-story bunker in the Hispanic ghetto in Proctor."

"I thought all of Proctor was an Hispanic ghetto," Susan said.

"San Juan Hill is a sub-ghetto," I said.

"Tell me about it," Susan said.

Which, with an interruption to order chicken pie for me, and a tossed salad, dressing on the side, for Susan, I did.

"And you have your translator, this Rollo man?"

"Chollo," I said.

"Yes. Is he good?"

"Very," I said.

"Does Frank know any of this?" Susan said.

"No. Even if I told him he'd forget it."

"When you tell him, how will he be?"

"He'll manage," I said. "Belson's a tough guy and he had a long unhappy first marriage, so he learned how to dull his feelings."

Susan smiled.

"Might be why he was always such a good cop," she said. "The wound and the bow."

"Disability of some kind helps strengthen us in other areas?"

Susan nodded. The waitress brought Susan her salad, and me the pot pie and another beer. Susan took a spray of red lettuce leaf from her salad and

dipped it delicately into the dressing on the side and nibbled on the end of
it.

"Save some room for dessert," I said.

"Don't you think the romantic make-believe about having no past
should have bothered Frank? Wouldn't it strike you as odd? It sounds cute,
but can you imagine us never saying anything about before?"

"Well," I said, "I don't know much about your ex-husband."

"Yes, but you know I have one."

I nodded.

"Belson's a smart cop, and he's been one for a long time," I said. "It
would strike him as odd too."

"If there is a silence," Susan said, "it is often the result of an unspoken
conspiracy, maybe even an unconscious conspiracy to keep something
under cover."

"You think Belson knew?" I said.

"He may not even know what she's concealing, only that there's something, and he doesn't want either of them to have to look."

The waitress came by to see if everything was all right. We said yes, and
Susan ordered a chicken sandwich, plain, no mayo, just bread and sliced
chicken. I raised my eyebrows.

"This is nearly gluttonous," I said. "A salad and a chicken sandwich?"

"The sandwich is for the baby," Susan said, "on the ride home."

"Of course," I said.

"Sometimes," Susan said, "when people have been, ah, unlucky in love,
so to speak, they are so fragile, and so untrusting of themselves, or of the
experience, that they want everything to remain in stasis. Be very careful.
Take no chances. You know? So they ask no questions."

"Yeah. Belson says he knows her better than anyone, even though he
knows nothing of her past."

"Maybe he does, but the fact that he thinks so doesn't make it so," Susan
said. "Love often makes us think things that aren't in fact so."

"I sometimes think I know you entirely," I said.

"You know me better than anyone ever has," Susan said.

"And yet you're quite secretive," I said. "You surprise me often."

"And hope to again," Susan said.

"Are you implying some sort of kinky sexual surprise?" I said.

Susan smiled a wide, friendly smile at me.

"Why yes," she said. "I am."

Chapter 30

Cholllo and I sat with Delaney, the Proctor Chief of Detectives, and two Proctor uniforms: a big jowly cop named Murphy, who had a lot of broken veins in his face, and a body builder named Sheehan, whose long black hair stuck out from under his uniform cap. The cap itself seemed too small for all that hair. It sat on top of it, as if he were the cop in a clown act.

"Okay," Delaney was saying, "you got no probable cause, okay? But the broad's husband is a brother officer, and you used to be a brother officer, so I send a couple people down to take a peek. No warrant, nothing. But my guys know their way around and they have a few words with the guy at the door and they go in. They talk to Luis Deleon, they talk to some of his people. They look around. There's no Anglo woman there."

Delaney gave a big sad shrug.

"You look everywhere?" I said.

"Hey, pal, this ain't Boston," Murphy said. "But it's not like we don't know our job."

"Your job is shaking down small-time junkies," I said. "I didn't say you don't know it."

"Is that a crack, Mister?" Delaney said.

"Anybody you talked to speak English?" I said.

"Deleon," Sheehan said. He sounded thrilled that he'd thought of someone.

"Anybody else?"

"They said no, but they understand when they want to," Murphy said. "Besides, we speak some Spanish."

"Chollo," I said. "Speak to them in Spanish."

Chollo was behind us, languidly holding up the wall. With no expression on his face, Chollo rattled off several sentences in Spanish. The three Proctor cops looked at him blankly.

"We're the cops here," Delaney said. "We don't have to take no fucking test. We say she ain't in there, you can take it or leave it."

I looked at Delaney for a time. Delaney tried to hold my gaze but couldn't. He looked down, then looked very quickly at his desk drawer, and away.

"We done what we could do," he said.

He took his bottle out of the desk drawer and fiddled with the cap.

I kept my gaze on Delaney.

"Lemme see if I got this straight. You sent these two twerps in to ask Deleon if he kidnapped Lisa St. Claire. Deleon says no, probably dukes them a twenty, and they tip their caps and say thank you, Jefe, and go get somebody to count it for them."

"Hey, pal," Sheehan said. "You're a fucking civilian and you're not even from here. We don't have to take any shit from you."

"The hell you don't," I said.

"Settle down," Delaney said. "We done what we can do without a warrant." He spoke very fast and his voice was sort of squeaky. "And I can't get no judge in the district to give me one on what you got."

He took a drink from the neck of the bottle.

"Now that's the fucking long and short of it," he said. "Lemme buy you a drink."

I shook my head.

"You ever see McGruff the crime dog?" I said. "Look out, because he'll want to take a bite out of you."

I turned and walked out of the office with Chollo behind me.

"Fucking McGruff the crime dog?" Chollo said.

"They can't all be winners," I said.

Chapter 31

He was waiting in the hallway outside my office when I got there in the morning. At first I didn't recognize him. He was wearing a black felt hat and a shabby old raincoat and looking furtive and ill at ease, so I figured he was a client.

"I'm Spenser," I said. "Are you looking for me?"

"Yes, you remember me? Father Ahearn from Proctor?"

"Of course, the hat and the coat fooled me. I thought you were out of uniform."

I unlocked the office door and we went in. The priest put his hat on the edge of my desk and sat uneasily on the front edge of one of my client chairs. Hawk always said that the presence of four client chairs in my office was the embodiment of foolish optimism.

"Want some coffee, Father?"

The priest hesitated as if I'd asked him too hard a question. Then he nodded.

"Decaf if you have it," the priest said.

"You're in luck, Father. I'm a decaf man myself."

Susan had given me a Mr. Coffee machine for the office to help me in my long-standing quest for decaffeination. I put some ground decaf in the basket, added the water, and turned it on. Then I went around my desk and opened the window a little so that fresh, or at least different, air could drift in from the Back Bay. Then I sat down at my desk.

"What can I do for you, Father?"

"You are still looking for the Anglo woman in Proctor?"

"Lisa St. Claire," I said.

The priest frowned slightly as if I'd given the wrong answer.

"Do you still think she is with Luis Deleon?"

"I think she might be, Father."

The priest was silent. The coffeemaker stopped gurgling and I got up and poured us two cups of coffee.

"Got sugar and condensed milk," I said.

"Just black, thank you."

I handed him a mug, added sugar and canned milk to mine, and took it back to my desk. I had a sip, it wasn't bad. Once you got over thinking it was going to be coffee and started thinking of it as a hot drink for mornings, it wasn't so disappointing. Some donuts would have helped. On the other hand, I couldn't think of anything some donuts wouldn't help. The priest blew on the surface of his coffee for a moment, then took a sip.

"I have been asked to publish the banns of marriage," he said, "on behalf of Luis Deleon and Angela Richard."

Bingo!

"Do you know Angela Richard?" I said.

"No. But I am scheduled to marry them."

"You've not met her?"

"No."

"Who asked you?"

"Luis Deleon came himself."

"Alone?"

"No, there were some other men with him."

"But without the bride-to-be," I said.

"Yes."

"Isn't that unusual?"

"Yes."

"Don't you usually want to see both of them and counsel them on the high seriousness of holy matrimony?"

"That is customary."

"Did he show you a marriage license?"

"No."

"Can you marry him legally without one?"

"No."

"So does he have one? Why didn't the bride-to-be come along? Why aren't they doing their prenuptial counseling?"

"I don't know," the priest said. "You do not question Luis Deleon about things."

"You don't," I said. "I might."

The priest shrugged.

"It is your work," he said.

It might have been his too, but I let it slide. He seemed to know his failings already. And the knowledge had not made him happy.

"When did Deleon come to see you?"

"Ten days ago."

"Took you a while to get here," I said.

"Yes. I was afraid."

"And now you're not?"

"No. I am still afraid. But, I . . . I felt I had to come here and tell you."

"Where will the ceremony take place?"

"At Luis Deleon's home."

"In San Juan Hill?"

"Yes."

"When the time comes, could you bring another priest with you?"

"Another priest?"

"Yeah."

"There is no need for another priest."

"I was thinking about me in a priest suit," I said.

The priest stared at me as if I were the anti-Christ.

"You think Angela Richard might be the other woman?"

"Could be," I said. No sense burdening the priest with more information than he can use.

"Holy Mother," he said.

"Could it be done?"

"A second priest? You in disguise? I . . . I don't know. I think . . . I think I would be . . . too . . . afraid."

"Sure," I said. "Is there anything else you can tell me?"

"No. It is all I know."

I nodded. We drank our coffee in silence.

"Does this information help you?" the priest said finally.

"All information helps," I said. "Once we figure out how it fits with other information."

"Maybe it means that the woman you seek is not there?"

"Maybe," I said. "Or maybe it is the woman I seek."

"She is already married."

"Yeah."

"Then how could I marry them?"

"Maybe they plan to lie," I said.

"Why would they do that?" the priest said.

"Maybe she has no choice," I said.

We drank our coffee again. The priest was thinking.

"I do not know what is right here. I was very afraid to come to you, afraid Luis Deleon would find out. But I came because I thought it was the right thing, and it would clear my conscience. Now I find that it opens up a multitude of things that are not right. What if Luis Deleon asks me to perform an illicit marriage? I hope it is not the same woman."

I made no comment.

"I hope that is the case," the priest said. "Is it selfish of me to wish that? It would mean that you have no idea where the missing woman is, and you have been wasting your time. It might mean that she is dead somewhere. Can I wish such a thing?"

"You're a man, Father. You probably can't always control what you wish."

"But I must try," the priest said. "I am not just a man. I am a man of God."

I looked at him sitting rigidly on the edge of my client chair, holding his half-empty cup of bad decaf, struggling with his soul. It must have been a struggle that occupied him daily.

"It took courage to come here and tell me this stuff, Father."

"Thank you," he said. He stood and took his coffee cup to my sink and rinsed it out and put it on the little table beside the Mr. Coffee.

"You'll let me know, Father, anything develops?"

"Yes."

"I'll check in with you in a while," I said.

"Of course."

"If it matters," I said, "you seem a pretty good man to me."

The priest smiled softly. He picked his hat up off my desk and put it square on his head. Nothing rakish.

"Thank you," he said. "I will talk with my confessor."

He went out of the office and closed the door very quietly behind him. I stood up and rinsed out my coffee cup and put it on the table beside his. Then I walked over and looked out my window and thought about what the priest had told me. As I stood, he came out the side door of my building, walked to the corner, and started up Boylston Street. He had his hands thrust deep into his raincoat pockets. His collar was turned up despite the sunshine, and his head was down. He wasn't finding a lot of joy in this world. For his sake I hoped he might be right about the next one.

Chapter 32

Chollo and I were back outside the Deleon complex, parked in a different spot. It was cold for spring and the partial sun was overmatched by the hard wind that kicked the gutter trash along the street. Styrofoam cups, hamburger boxes, plastic cup lids, beer cans, the indestructible filter tips of disintegrated cigarettes, scraps of newspaper, bottle caps, match books, gum wrappers, and discolored food cartons with bent wire handles were tumbled about fitfully by the erratic wind. I could hear road sand and grit propelled by the wind, pinging against the car.

"Angela is the same as Lisa?" Chollo said. "Right?"

"And she's not there voluntarily," I said. "You ever hear of a couple getting married and only the guy goes to visit the priest?"

"You think he used her other name so when the banns were announced, nobody will know?"

"Maybe."

"So why announce the banns?" Chollo said.

"Propriety," I said.

"And you think he's holding her?"

"Yeah."

"And he's forcing her to marry him, even though she's married already to another guy?"

"Yeah."

"And he's going to the priest and publishing the fucking banns?"

I stared at the moldering tenements and took a slow breath.

"Yeah," I said. "That's what I think."

"That's fucking crazy, man."

I nodded, still looking at the blank gray clapboard buildings across the street.

"Yeah," I said. "It is."

We were quiet for a while, listening to the wind, looking at the tenements.

"And you are sure it's your friend's wife in there?"

"Yeah."

"Enough fucking broads in the world," Chollo said. "Free for the taking. Don't make much sense to go stealing one from some guy. Especially, the guy's a cop."

"Makes sense if you're crazy," I said.

"And you figure he's crazy and he's got the cop's wife."

"It's an explanation," I said.

"Be nice we knew what the setup in there was," Chollo said. "Case we decide to go in and get her."

"Yeah."

A dog trotted by, head down, ears back, busy, on his way somewhere. He was a street dog, so mongrelized after generations of street breeding that he barely looked like a dog. He looked more like something wild, some kind of Ur-dog—the original pattern, maybe, that had existed before the cave men started to pat them.

"I think I'll go in, take another look around."

"You going to tell them you're the tooth fairy making a delivery?" I said.

"I will tell them I work for Vincent del Rio, who is an important man in Los Angeles."

The way he said Los Angeles reminded me that, despite the unaccented English, Chollo was Mexican.

"Yeah?"

"I will say that Mr. del Rio is seeking an East Coast associate for some of his enterprises. And that he has sent me here to assess Luis Deleon's setup. I will explain this is why I have been sitting outside here," Chollo grinned at me, "with my driver."

"Not bad," I said. "They don't know me, why don't I go in with you?"

Chollo shook his head.

"No gringos," Chollo said. "On the first visit. Except to drive the car, and maybe shoot a little. Nobody will talk to me if I come in with a gringo."

"Gee," I said. "That sounds kind of racially insensitive to me."

Chollo grinned.

"Sí, señor," he said.

"What if they insist on a phone call to del Rio?"

"I have already spoken to Mr. del Rio," Chollo said. "He is prepared to support my story."

"So, you're not making this up as you go along," I said.

"No. I do that only when I have to."

"Which is often," I said.

Chollo nodded.

"Which is often."

He opened the door on his side, and put one foot out.

"Don't get cute in there," I said. "I don't want the woman to get hurt."

"I shall be as sly as a Yucatan tree toad," Chollo said.

"Are they really sly?" I said.

"I don't know, I just made it up," Chollo said.

He got out of the car and turned up the collar of his jacket as he walked across the street, squinting against the grit that the wind was tossing. He went up the steps of the tenement and talked to the guard. The guard listened and talked and listened and talked. Then he turned and went in. Chollo waited in the doorway, shielded from the wind. In a little while the door opened and the guard came back out. With him was the slim guy with braids. The three of them talked for several minutes. Then Chollo and the guy with braids went back inside and the guard remained.

The slim young woman in the pink sweatshirt came into her room with one of the men she'd seen guarding her door. The woman was carrying a small plastic shopping bag. She pointed toward the chair.

"You want me to sit in the chair?" she said.

The woman pointed toward the chair again. There was a quality of triumph in her bearing.

"Why? Why do you want me to sit in the chair?" Lisa said.

The woman shrugged and said something to the man in Spanish. Each of them took hold of an arm and they forced her backwards and sat her on the chair. While the man held Lisa in the chair, the woman took some clothesline from the plastic bag and tied Lisa's hands to the chair behind her and squatted and tied her ankles to the chair legs. In each case she yanked at the ropes and tied them too tight.

"Why, you bastards! Why are you tying me up?" Lisa said. "Don't, please, don't tie me up. Please! I don't want to be tied. Please, you're hurting me. I . . ."

The woman said something in Spanish to her and laughed. She took some gray duct tape from her bag and forced it against Lisa's mouth angrily and taped it shut, wrapping the tape an extra vengeful turn around Lisa's head. She stood back in front of Lisa and looked at her tied to the chair and laughed and put her hand on her own crotch and said something angrily to Lisa in Spanish. The man stepped to her side and said something. She gestured him away. He spoke to her again more forcefully, and she shrugged and took a portable radio out of her plastic bag and put it on the table near Lisa, turned it on, and turned the volume up. It was a Spanish language station. Salsa music filled the room. The woman folded the plastic bag and put it on the table beside the radio. She stopped again in front of Lisa and stared at her, as if she savored Lisa's helplessness. Then she put her hand under Lisa's chin and raised Lisa's face and spat in it. The man spoke to her sharply and the woman laughed and she and the man left the room. Lisa could hear the door lock behind them. She felt the claustrophobic panic begin to seep through her. The woman's spittle trickled down her cheek. She struggled frantically for a moment. There was no give in the rope. Calm, she thought. Calm. I got through it before. Why did they do it? I can't get out anyway. The door's locked and there's a guard. Why tie me up? Why gag me? No one can hear me. Is he someplace? Taking pictures?

What the hell is the radio for? To drown out noise? How can I make noise? You couldn't hear me five feet away with my mouth taped . . . There's someone in the building. She felt a sudden stab of excitement. That's it, there's someone here. She started again to struggle with the ropes. But she was helpless. The woman had tied her feet to the legs of the chair in such a way that her feet were off the floor. She had no leverage. The knots were hard. She couldn't get free. She couldn't make noise. Calm, she thought. Calm. Calm. When they're gone he'll cut you loose. He'll come back. Why was that woman so cruel? Luis will come back and untie me. He'll protect me. She sat perfectly still and focused on her breath going in and out. And in a while she was calm. She was uncomfortable. The ropes were too tight. But she was not in actual pain. How quickly we learn to settle for less, she thought. Getting control of herself was her first triumph since he'd taken her. Maybe not the last one, she thought. She relaxed herself into the ropes and the chair, making her body go slack, letting her head drop. Breathing quietly. She realized that Luis was beginning to seem her protector, that she looked forward to his return. She remembered her iron pipe hidden under her mattress. She thought about it. It was like a treasure to savor. I won't always be tied up, she thought, as she sat helpless and relaxed. I won't always be tied up.

Chapter 33

I took out the Browning nine millimeter I was carrying and put it on the car seat beside my leg. I started the car up and let it idle, just in case we needed to leave suddenly, and then settled back against the car seat to wait. From where I sat, I could slouch down and see a man moving on the roof top of one of the tenements. He wore a red plaid shirt. From my angle it was hard to tell for sure, but he seemed to be carrying a rifle or a shotgun. The windows in the room below him were closed up with plywood. He moved away from my side of the roof and I couldn't see him anymore. The dog that had trotted by earlier returned, going in the other direction. Another dog was with him. It didn't really look like him, but it was the same kind of atavistic mongrel, middle-sized and light brown, with its tail arching over its back. The two of them turned a corner and disappeared behind the tenement complex. I looked back up at the roof. The guy with the red plaid shirt was back. This time I could see that it was in fact a long gun he carried, though I couldn't make out whether it was a rifle or a shotgun. Given the range, I was hoping for a shotgun, in case Chollo's story didn't convince anyone and they decided to shoot at me. In the distance, east of Proctor, the scattered clouds were starting to coalesce, and the distance looked dark. It would probably rain in a while. The atmosphere had the heavy feel of it, and wind from the east, off the ocean, usually brought rain with it at this time of year. Now that the dogs were gone, the street was empty. No traffic moved through the neighborhood. No ice cream trucks, no police cars, no women pushing babies in carriages with the clear plastic rain shields down. When the rain came it killed the wind. I could see it falling before it reached me. I watched it march toward me up the silent street, falling straight down, a thin, beaded curtain of it, turning the pavement dark as it came. When it hit the car, I turned the windshield wipers on *intermittent,* just enough so I could see if anyone was coming toward me with a gun.

The guy on the roof had disappeared, probably inside someplace or under something. If we ever had to take a run at the place it might be good to wait till it rained. Nothing happened. No one moved. Time trudged past me very slowly. I started to make a list of all the women I'd slept with in my life, trying to remember all the circumstances. I wondered if it was disloyal to Susan, and found myself thinking about whether it was or not, rather than with whom I had done what. Maybe she thought about the people she'd slept with. How did I feel? I decided I didn't mind, unless she thought of them with longing. So I went back to remembering my sex life, but I was careful not to long for anyone. The rain was harder now, too hard for *intermittent.* I changed it. I looked at my watch. Chollo had been in there for forty minutes.

I thought about Brenda Loring. She was a nice woman. She had great thighs. I liked her. But I loved Susan. Through the clear wiper arc on the windshield I saw Chollo come out of the tenement and walk toward the car. He seemed to be in no hurry. But he would look like he wasn't in a hurry if he was being chased by a bull. I glanced at my watch again. An hour and five minutes.

Chollo got in the car and closed the door behind him.

"How'd it go?" I said.

Chollo grinned.

"Luis embraced me when I left."

"How sweet," I said.

"You cold gringos don't understand us hot-blooded Latinos," Chollo said.

"You want to wait for your blood to cool," I said, "before you fill me in?"

"Lunch," Chollo said. "First I need lunch."

"Maybe I can find a Jack in the Box," I said.

"My native cuisine," Chollo said. "How thoughtful."

I turned on the headlights and put the car in gear and we drove away.

I mages of herself tied to the chair were added to the other images on the monitors that glowed soundlessly in the dim room. He had come in with his video camera and videotaped before he cut her loose.

"It is business, querida. I am sorry it had to be this way. But I cannot trust you yet not to be crazy. Let me get some skin cream for you, where the tape was."

I can control myself, she thought. If I can do that, I can do anything.

"Who was here?" she said.

"There were important people here, Angela, they have sought me out. They want me to help them here with their business. They admire me. But why should you think about business? Your beautiful head should be thinking beautiful thoughts."

"So why didn't you want them to know about me? What are you afraid of, if they are such good friends of yours?"

"People should know of me and my business only what they need to know," Luis said. "Only what I choose for them to know."

"Who was that woman who tied me up?"

"Rosalita," he said. "She is nothing. She has always thought I belonged to her."

He paused as he spoke, watching the latest videotape.

"I'm sorry, chiquita, that you had to be tied."

"No," she said, herself surprised at the strength of her voice. "No, you're not sorry. You'd like me bound and gagged for you all the time."

"What can you be saying? Did I not rush in here and untie you as soon as I could?"

"Don't be so literal. Don't you understand that the image of your feeling for me is embodied in those tapes, the picture of me bound and helpless, hauled in here on a dolly, tied and gagged when there's visitors. I'm yours in a way that offers me no choices."

"There are pictures of you and me at the beach," he said. "Pictures of you and me on stage."

"You don't want a lover, you want a slave."

"Angel, I am your slave."

He was beginning to pace again.

"Since my mother . . . Wait, let me show you. You've never seen my mother."

He disappeared behind one of the theatrical flats, and in a moment the image on the monitors changed. There was a picture of a young Hispanic woman. Long dark hair, high breasts, black tank top, white miniskirt, white boots. The camera movements were sudden and jerky. The images were slightly indistinct, and the color was odd, like a colorized movie, but she could see how much she looked like Luis.

"It is my mother," he said. "Isn't she beautiful?"

Too much makeup, Lisa thought. Hair's too big, skirt's too tight.

"She gave me the camera, an eight millimeter. She taught me how to use it."

The camera steadied and then a young boy came into the picture. He put his arm around his mother's waist. She put her arm around his shoulder, and they stood and smiled into the camera.

"And that is me, with my mother," he said.

The scene cut clumsily to another picture. The same woman, dressed differently, but no better, Lisa thought. She was sitting on the lap of a heavy-set, red-faced Anglo man in a loud sport coat. Her short skirt was high on her thighs and the man's hand rested on the inner part of her thigh above the knee.

"That is a friend of my mother's," Luis said. "My mother had many friends."

The woman in the camera smiled and gestured at the camera to stop filming. It kept on, and then stopped abruptly.

"I took all the old films and had them transferred to video," Luis said. "That way even though she's gone I will have her still."

Chapter 34

There was a Subway sandwich shop in a shopping center off Route 93, a little west of Proctor. I pulled in and parked in front of it. Chollo looked at the sandwich shop.

"What's this," Chollo said, "your native cuisine?"

"Good Yankee cookin'," I said.

"Get me a ham and cheese sub," Chollo said. "No hot peppers."

"No hot peppers?"

Chollo shrugged.

"Now and then," he said, "I am untrue to my heritage."

"Hell," I said. "It happens. I don't always eat potatoes."

"Cultural genocide," Chollo said.

I went into the shop and bought us a couple of sandwiches and some coffee and came back. Chollo took a sip of coffee and made a face.

"What the fuck is this?" he said.

"You must have got mine," I said and we swapped.

"You drink that?" Chollo said.

"You get used to it."

"Why would you want to?"

"You may have a point," I said. "What went on in the house?"

Chollo put his coffee into one of the holders in the middle console and began to unwrap his sandwich.

"They bought my story," Chollo said. "Deleon knew of Mr. del Rio. I told him we had talked with Freddie Santiago, but we weren't happy. Said Freddie looked kind of tired to me. Said Mr. del Rio and me thought we might need a younger guy, some fresh blood to run this end."

Chollo picked up half of his sub sandwich and took a bite. He managed not to get any on himself, and I wondered how he did it. Susan always claimed that when I ate a sub I looked like I'd fought with it. He chewed happily. I waited. The hot coffee steamed the inside of the windshield a little so that the only clear reality seemed to be here in the car, where the food was.

"Deleon liked that," Chollo said. "Got him excited. Says he's just the man for the job. Says he's got the perfect setup. So I say, lemme take a look around, see what you got here, and we take a tour."

Chollo drank some coffee. I waited.

"Three things," Chollo said. "One, Deleon's a froot loop. Two, there's a locked room with a guard outside on the second floor. It would be the corner on the second floor, where the windows are covered with plywood. Guard pretended he was just hanging around, but he was guarding. And there's a new padlock on the door. I said to Deleon, 'What's in there?' and he says it's his private quarters. Says 'I alone have the key.' Like fucking Basil Rathbone, you know? Except he's speaking Spanish with a Puerto Rican accent."

The good thing about listening instead of talking is you can eat while you do it. I was finished with my sandwich, Chollo just took his second bite.

"What's number three?" I said.

"Walls are sandbagged, windows are all wire-meshed or boarded over. There's a lot of ammunition, lot of food. For crissake, they got a garden on the roof, maybe a dozen shooters, plus women and kids. Buildings are all connected through sheltered access. We gotta go in there we can do it, but I don't see how we do it without we blow up some women and kids."

"Probably why they're there," I said.

"Now that's cynical," Chollo said. "Nothing as cynical as a cynical Yankee."

"Yeah, you're probably right," I said. "Why do you think they're there?"

"To keep people from assaulting the place for fear of killing the kids," Chollo said.

I nodded.

"Of course," I said. "You say they got a garden on the roof? Stuff grow in pots or what?"

"No, they dumped a bunch of dirt up there, must have carried it up in buckets. It's a flat roof and it's covered with dirt and there's a bunch of plants growing up there."

"What kind?"

"I look like fucking Juan Valdez?" Chollo said. "How the fuck do I know what kind? I was twenty-three before I found out that stuff didn't grow canned."

"House is supporting a lot of weight," I said. "How about Deleon? What do you think?"

"Deleon's not normal," Chollo said.

"You mentioned that," I said.

"He walks around in there like he's on the Starship Enterprise. And he dresses like he's going to a masquerade. He had some kind of fucking vaquero look today—boots, the whole deal. Even carried a short leather whip around his wrist. Like a quirt, you know. Like he was Gilbert Roland."

"Theatrical," I said.

"Absolutely, and he can't wait for you to stop talking so he can tell you some more about himself. My people this, and my operation that, and my citadel so and so. He actually uses the word *citadel,* for crissake."

"You think she's in there?" I said.

"I didn't see her," Chollo said.

"But there's a locked room."

"Yeah, there is."

"And there are wedding plans."

"Yeah, there are."

We sat quietly for a while. Chollo finished his sandwich and I drank some decaf while he did it. Chollo finished his sandwich, wiped his mouth carefully with a paper napkin, put the napkin in the bag the sandwich had come in, and sat back to drink his coffee. There was no hint of pickle juice on his shirt.

"He's such a jelly bean," Chollo said. "He could have his private quarters guarded to make himself feel, like, important."

"And the wedding?"

"Could be the lovely bride is filming in Monaco," Chollo said, "and jetting in just before the event."

"And hubby-to-be is arranging the wedding."

"Sure," Chollo said.

"You believe that?"

"No."

"You think she's in there?"

"Somebody is," Chollo said.

"So we gotta go in."

"Going to be a lot of blood we go in there straight on," Chollo said. "I got no problem with that, but if it is Belson's wife is in there, he might."

"We gotta go in," I said.

*S*he was a princess, a wonderful mother," Luis said. "She was beautiful and she cared for me beyond all else."

As he spoke, the badly edited film jerked from scene to scene. In many of the scenes, lit by the cheap floodlight bar of his camera, Luis's mother was with men. In one scene she was kissing a man next to a bed when she was filmed. The man had a hand on her butt. The fabric of her short skirt was gathered in his hand. The skirt was hiked nearly hip high. She turned as if frightened, holding her hand to shield her face, gesturing at the camera.

"I used to tease her when she would come home with a date. I would catch her giving them a little kiss and later I would tease her about it. But it was never anything with the men. She always said I was the only one, the man she truly loved."

"And your father?"

Luis shook his head, annoyed.

"I had no father," he said.

"Is he alive?"

"I told you," he said, "I have no father."

The film looped back to the beginning, and began its second runthrough. The apartment so often pictured seemed no more than a single room. The men pictured were never the same.

"Your mother had a lot of men," Lisa said.

"They were friends. She never loved them."

"She had friends in every night?"

Luis stood suddenly, and walked to the far side of the room.

"Did they stay all night?" Lisa asked.

"We will not speak anymore of my mother," Luis said. "We will talk of other things."

He walked back behind the theater flats for a moment. She could feel his weakness, and she could feel her strength.

"Did they stay all night?"

He reappeared. When he spoke his voice was low and firm and dangerous, like a movie villain.

"We will talk of us, now," he said.

"Your mother was a hooker, wasn't she?" Lisa said.

Luis whirled toward her and slapped her hard across the face; she fell to *her hands and knees. Her head ringing. And from that position she heard herself laughing.*

"She was, wasn't she? She was."

And then Luis was on his knees beside her crying, his arms around her.

"I am sorry, Angel, I am sorry. I am so sorry."

She raised her head and looked at him, still on hands and knees, and saw the tears, and laughed. The sound of it ugly even to her.

"Hell, Luis," she said. "So was I."

Chapter 35

Deleon look like his mug shot?" I said.

"Yeah, but real tall," Chollo said.

"Six-five," I said. "What do you think?"

"He's dangerous, but he's not tough, you know. He's like a big kid and he's full of himself, but he's not really sure, and he's afraid someone will find him out, and you know he's kind of desperate all the time. He's got that look you see in some of the gang kids, the new ones. They're scared, but they're crazy, and they'd die to get respect, so you don't know what they'll do. You can't trust them not to be stupid."

I nodded.

"That's what Deleon's like. Guys like you and me, we know pretty well what we can do if we need to. Don't spend a lot of time thinking about it. Don't care too much if other people know it. Deleon doesn't know what he can do, or if he can do it, and he wants everyone to think he does and can, if you see what I'm saying. If the woman wasn't involved, he'd be easy enough. I've made a good living putting guys in the ground that were trying to prove how dangerous they were because they weren't sure themselves."

"But the woman is involved."

"Yeah, and that makes Deleon dangerous as a bastard because you can't do it simple, and you can't do anything without knowing how it'll affect the woman, and you can't trust him to do anything that makes any sense to you. And he's big and he's got a gun."

"Swell," I said. "Is there a number-two man?"

Chollo laughed.

"El Segundo is a skinny little shooter with a big long ponytail, named Ramon Gonzalez. A coke head, got a thin, droopy moustache, jitters around behind Deleon wearing two guns."

Chollo laughed again.

"I don't mean a gun and some sort of hide-out piece in an ankle holster. Or a back-up under your arm. I mean he's wearing two Sig Sauer nines with custom grips, one on each hip, like the fucking Frito bandito."

"He a real shooter?" I said.

"Oh yeah," Chollo said. "And he loves Luis. Looks at him like he was George fucking Washington."

"I never been too scared of a guy wears two guns," I said.

"How many people you met wear two guns?"

"The only other one is Hoot Gibson," I said.

"I don't know if he's good, but Ramon's real. I know the type. He shoots people 'cause he likes it."

"And you don't," I said.

"I got no feelings about it," Chollo said. "I do it 'cause they pay me."

"I'm not paying you," I said.

Chollo grinned.

"Maybe I'll go to heaven," he said.

"You got my word on it," I said. "There's a dozen shooters? That include Deleon and Gonzalez?"

"I don't know. It's an estimate. I counted nine while I was in there plus Deleon and Gonzalez. Figured there were a few I missed, on the roof maybe, growing squashes. So twelve, fifteen guys altogether."

"And the women and children are theirs?"

"Sure. The place is broken up into apartments with a common kitchen, looks like. Floor plan doesn't make any sense."

"That'd be perfect. Nothing else makes any sense. I don't know if she's in there, and if she is I don't know why. And the only way to find out is to go in, but if I go she may get killed."

"Hey, señor," Chollo said. "I'm just the translator. I am not paid to theenk."

"Lucky for you," I said.

The coffee was gone and the sandwiches were eaten. I gathered up the debris and got out and dumped it in a waste barrel near the sub shop. It was a fine bright spring day with the sun reflecting off the parked cars and glinting on their chrome trim, and sparkling off the tiny flecks of mica in the surface of the parking lot. Adolescent girls in striped tee shirts and cut-off jeans loitered along under the arcade roof that ran along the front of the shopping center. Most of them smoked. Some of them inhaled. One of them saw me looking at them and stared back at me, full of bravado and uncertainty, and straightened slightly so that her new bosom, about which she was doubtless uneasy, stuck out proudly. I grinned at her, and she turned away quickly.

Ah sweet bird of youth. They used to come running when I smiled.

Back in the car I started up and headed back up Route 93.

"What now, Jefe?" Chollo said.

"Thought we'd go back and park in a different place and look at the citadel some more."

"Man, it's amazing to watch an ace detective work," Chollo said.

"Think how it is to be one," I said.

We drove for a while in silence, Chollo looking at the bland, semirural scenery along the road. When we got to San Juan Hill, I parked on a different corner facing the other way. They had made no improvements in the property while we were gone.

"How long we going to look at this fucking rat hole?" Chollo said.

"Until I figure out how to get in there and get her out."

Chollo eased lower in the seat and let his chin rest on his chest.

"That long," he said.

They sat beside each other on the floor. He was still teary, but he listened as she talked.

"I didn't grow up in Los Angeles," she said. "I grew up in Haverhill. My old man was a drunk and a bum and a womanizer. He left my mother when I was about ten. My mother got custody, but my father came back and got me and took me with him. Kidnapped me, more or less. I don't think he even wanted me so much as he didn't want my mother to have me. I spent a couple years hiding in the backseat of his car, or sneaking into motel rooms after dark so no one would see me. I didn't go to school or play with other kids. My father, when he was sober, would pick up odd jobs and leave me alone during the day when he did them. I watched TV. Eventually some private detective my mother hired found me and kidnapped me back. My mother never forgave my father for cheating on her and leaving her, and she never forgave me, probably, for being his daughter. All the rest of my growing up I heard about what a wretch he was, what wretches all men were. I probably never forgave my father for letting them take me back."

"But your mother loved you," Luis said.

The flashes of naivete had always appealed to her, innocence shining through the machismo and flash. Probably because it was real, she thought. The rest was posture, and she always knew that it was. But in those days the innocence had once redeemed it.

"No," Lisa said, "my mother definitely did not love me. I was pretty much just another one of my father's women to her. She assumed from the moment I reached puberty that I was a disgusting slut, like all the rest of them."

"You should not speak this way about your mother," Luis said. He was leaning forward now toward her, his forearms resting on his thighs. He was listening so hard he seemed to be watching her lips as they formed the words.

"It's the truth," she said. "To be sane, you have to know the truth and be able to say it."

"My poor Angel," Luis said. "It must have been horrible to have such a mother."

"Yeah, well, I didn't stick around too long. When I was seventeen, I took off with a local guy named Woody Pontevecchio. Woody had some money he'd stolen and we hitchhiked mostly, all the way across the country. We *were going, guess where, to Hollywood. He was going to manage me and I was going to be a star."*

"You are certainly beautiful enough," Luis said.

"Sure. I was beautiful in Haverhill. In Hollywood, everybody's beautiful. I had as much chance as a cow."

"But you are so talented."

"Yeah. We had a room in a flop house in Venice, with a toilet down the hall. I got a job as a waitress in one of the joints on the beach, and Woody started hustling Hollywood. At first he got me some gigs doing sexy DJ stuff at parties—you know, wearing a string bikini while I played records and did chit chat, then we developed an act where I'd show up to do DJ work all dressed up and through the evening I'd strip, one piece of clothing at a time. He billed me as Hollywood's only exotic disc jockey, and then sure enough, he finally got me a job in pictures."

"You have never told me this," Luis said. "You have never said any of this to me."

"Time I did," Lisa said. "I had a supporting role in a sixteen-millimeter film called Randy Pants."

"Randy Pants? *What kind of movie is that?"*

"Porno. I had a run of porn films for a while, but I was never any good at it, all that moaning and heavy breathing, and finally the parts stopped coming, and the exotic DJ schtick wasn't going anywhere, so Woody turned me out."

As she spoke, Luis was shaking his head, slowly, back and forth, as if he were trying to clear it.

"No," Luis said.

"Yeah, he did."

"No."

"Yeah. Like your old lady, Luis. I was a whore, just like your old lady."

"No," Luis said again. "No, no, no."

He was crying, and pounding both his fists on his thighs as he said "no," invoking the word like a chant as if to exorcise the truth.

"No, no, no, no . . ." And then the crying overcame the no. He slumped toward her and pressed his face against her and she put her arm around him and patted him softly as he wept.

"Me and your old lady, both," she said, "me and your old lady."

Chapter 36

It was getting dark.

Chollo eased into a more comfortable position on the front seat and said, "You think of anything yet?"

"If we're going to go in, we need a plan," I said.

"You think of that so quick?" Chollo said.

"Trained investigator," I said. "I know the place is a maze, but can you find the woman's room?"

"Sí."

"House has a stairwell in a front hall," I said. "I can see that from here. Probably designed originally as a three-family."

"How you tell?" Chollo said.

"My father was a carpenter," I said. "It's in the genes."

"Was he also an asshole?"

"No. That's an acquired trait," I said.

"Well, you're right. Woman's room is off the second-floor front hall. Should be where those windows are boarded up. There's a set of back stairs too. And a couple places where holes have been cut in the floor and ladders go down, or up, depending where you are."

"A nice amenity," I said.

We were quiet. The darkness settled slowly around us. Most of the street lights in San Juan Hill didn't work. The night sky was overcast. It was dark in the way it must have been dark in earlier times, except for some light that showed in the barricaded windows at the Deleon citadel.

"Who's going in?" Chollo said.

"You and me."

"How's your plan coming?" Chollo said.

"It's probably going to have something to do with me going in with you on the deal to make Deleon Mr. del Rio's East Coast marketing manager."

"I told you, no gringos. They won't buy it."

"How about I'm from the local mob, to discuss the territorial fee?"

"Isn't that Freddie Santiago?"

"I'm from Boston," I said. "Joe Broz sent me up to see where this fits in with us."

"Broz the stud duck around here?"

"Used to be," I said. "Thinks he is."

"What if Deleon checks with him?"

"Deleon probably can't get to Broz, but no harm being careful. Broz owes me a favor."

"You can get to Broz?"

"Yeah."

"You big with the bad guys, Spenser. You got Santiago helping you, Mr. del Rio helping you, now this guy Broz, that I don't know, he's helping you. And I'm helping you. You sure you are a good guy?"

"No," I said. "I'm not sure."

Chollo was silent in the almost perfect darkness next to me.

"Okay," he said after a while. "Say that works and it gets us in. Then what?"

"Then we improvise," I said.

"And you're sure she's in the castle there with Deleon?" Chollo said.

"Yes."

"What makes you so sure?"

"It makes more sense than anything else we can think of."

"And she's there against her will."

"She hasn't come out at all while we've been watching."

"Neither has he," Chollo said. "Maybe they are in there doing the funky chicken all the time."

"Possible."

"Once they ball one of us, you know," Chollo said, "they never want to fuck no gringo again."

"I didn't know that," I said.

Chollo grinned.

"Been my experience, at least."

"Funny," I said. "Mine's been different."

"Lot of broads take off on the old man. Don't say a word. Just get in the station wagon and go. The old man's walking around saying, 'She'd never do it. She don't even like sex.' And the old lady's banging some guy's ears off in a motel in El Monte."

"El Monte?" I said.

"Lotta people getting laid in El Monte," Chollo said.

"How nice for them," I said. "But we've played grab ass with this thing long enough. We got to go in."

In the darkness I could hear Chollo inhale quietly, a long breath which he let out slowly. We both sat in the near solid darkness staring at a house we could barely see, looking for a woman who might be there.

After a while Chollo said, "Works for me, Kemo Sabe."

do not know who my father was," he said.

He was not crying now, but his voice was still shaky and he spoke haltingly, sitting on the floor beside her, her arm around him, his head on her shoulder.

"My mother was with many men. Many Anglo men. My father might have been Anglo. My mother would bring them to our room because she had nowhere else to bring them. We had only a room, with a sink and a stove and a television. My mother hung up a blanket to hide my part of the room, but I could peek around, and I could hear, even when she turned up the television. I did not like being there, but I had nowhere else to go."

His breathing was short and he stared at the floor in front of them while she patted his shoulder.

"And afterwards my mother would say to me that she didn't love these men. She would say that she only loved me. But that the men had to come here and she had to pretend to love them. We could pretend too, she told me. We could pretend that we were living in a high room in a great castle. And we could pretend that the men were handsome knights who bravely stormed the castle and climbed up to the room to seek her hand in marriage."

"And that's what you pretended," she said.

"Yes."

They were quiet for a moment. She could feel tremors run through him as he breathed. The room was dim, and it smelled dank. She heard a sound that might have been rain falling outside the boarded windows.

"Every Sunday," he said, "she would take me to the movies. There were no men on Sundays. We would go sometimes to the movies all day. We loved the movies. It is why she bought me the camera. She said maybe I could be a movie person someday."

The pictures of his mother and the men she was with moved jerkily on the monitors. Luis stood up suddenly and disappeared behind the scenery. The monitors went black for the first time since she'd been in the room. Luis came back and stood looking at the blank screens. The room seemed dark without their glow . . . and damp. She shivered and hugged herself.

"How did she die, Luis?"

"She was killed by Freddie Santiago."

Chapter 37

It was 8:30 in the morning when we entered Club del Aguadillano. There were six people in the place, drinking beer mostly, though one guy appeared to be drinking tequila and washing it down with beer. Made decaf seem better. Even inside the club, you could smell the river smell lurking behind the beer smell, and hear the faint thunder of the falls upstream, as a kind of undertone to the harsh sounds of the juke box. Dolly the bartender was wearing an attractive green tee shirt today, with the sleeves cut off. His massive upper arms were illuminated with tattoos of intertwined figures. He studied us as we came in. Chollo spoke to him in Spanish and Dolly answered. He put two glasses up on the bar and poured some tequila in them. Then he walked down to the far end of the bar and stood, staring at nothing. Chollo and I ignored the tequila. After a while the guy with the tequila and beer stood up and yelled something in Spanish at one of the beer drinkers. The beer drinker muttered something back, and the tequila drinker started toward him. He was a squat guy with thick hands that suggested a lifetime of heavy labor. The beer drinker stood. He was a tallish guy, with a medium build. A very large and startling belly pushed incongruously out under his dingy white tee shirt like something he'd hidden under there. The tequila drinker grabbed him by the shirt front.

"They are arguing about whether the guy with the belly is a fucking faggot," Chollo murmured.

Without a word Dolly lumbered out from behind the bar. He took the sawed-off baseball bat out of his hip pocket and hit the tequila drinker hard behind the knees. The tequila drinker howled and fell over backwards. Dolly took him by the collar and dragged him howling to the front door, into the parking lot, dropped him, hit him hard once on each knee with the sawed-off bat and came back in, closing the door behind him. He put the sawed-off bat back into his hip pocket and went back behind the bar.

"Forceful," Chollo said.

"Well, he didn't bite him," I said.

"But, oh so gentle," Chollo said.

The door to Santiago's office opened and the gray-haired guy with the horn-rims nodded for us to enter.

Santiago was there, behind his desk. Besides the gray-haired man and Santiago there were four gunnies ranged on the back wall. One of them, the guy Chollo had knocked down last time, had a sawed-off shotgun in his hands. Nobody invited us to sit. The guy with the shotgun said something in Spanish to Chollo. Chollo smiled.

"He says if, this time, I would like to see if I can get my gun out before he pulls the trigger, he would be happy to try it."

Without looking at him, Santiago said, "Silencio!" to the guy with the shotgun.

"He's telling him to shut up," Chollo said.

"Is that what that means?" I said.

Santiago looked at me.

"You have a proposition?"

"If something happened to Luis Deleon, who would be in charge?" I said.

Santiago smiled.

"Eventually I would be."

"In the short run?" I said.

"Ramon Gonzalez, but he would not last very long."

"Because?"

"Because Ramon Gonzalez is a jitterbug, a man who runs on cocaine and angel dust. Luis is the one holds out against me. It is hatred, as if somehow it is my fault about his mother. If he were not there, sooner or later the others would be happy to join with me for a better Proctor."

Whatever he said was tinged with self-mockery so that it was never easy to know what he cared about and what he didn't. Which, I suppose, might have been the point.

"But they won't go against him?"

"They fear him more than they fear me. He is so crazy. It makes him"— he looked at Chollo—"*feroz?*"

"Ferocious," Chollo said.

"Sí, ferocious. Everyone is afraid of him, because he is so ferocious, and because no one knows what he will do. He is able to bring a lot of business in because so many fear him."

"What happened to his mother?" I said.

"She O.D.'d here, in the ladies' room," Santiago said. "Got hold of some uncut heroin and it popped her. Luis would not believe his mother was a junkie as he would not believe his mother was a whore. So he says I killed her." He shrugged. "Why would I bother to kill her? She was just a whore."

"One of yours?" I said.

Santiago smiled.

"Most things in Proctor are mine."

"Except San Juan Hill."

He nodded.

"Except that," he said softly.

"That could change," I said.

"All things do," Santiago said.

"We're going to take him out," I said.

"If you can."

"We can, but we'd like a little help from you."

"I do not wish to be seen as one who turns on a fellow Hispanic," Santiago said. "It would not help people to think of me as the liberator of Proctor."

"Of course it wouldn't," I said. "We'll be the ones who turn on him. What we want from you is logistical support."

"I could consider that," Santiago said. "Have you a plan?"

"Nothing so formal," I said. "But I've been thinking."

Santiago smiled.

"Tell me," he said.

"You tell him, Chollo, in Spanish. I want everything clear when the time comes. Give him the layout, make sure he knows where everyone is likely to be."

Chollo spoke in Spanish.

When he was through, Santiago said, "That is all? A show of force?"

"And nothing more. And when we say so," I said.

"Do you wish me to have the police to seal off the area?"

"You," I said. "Your people. I don't want the Proctor cops within a mile of the place."

"Certainly," Santiago said. "Will you tell me how this fits into your plan?"

"No," I said.

Santiago nodded.

"If I were you, I would say the same. Plans are best when few people know them."

"You are very wise, Jefe," I said.

Santiago smiled.

"Sí," he said. "But you should remember that I am a very vengeful man, and if things turn out to be different than you promised that they would be, I will find each of you and kill you . . ." He paused, made a searching gesture with his hand, and looked at Chollo.

"*Pavoroso?*"

Chollo grinned.

"Gruesome," he said. "Terrifying."

"Gee," I said. "I can't speak for everybody, but that sure seems fair to me."

"I enjoy laughter, too," Santiago said. "But don't mistake me."

"I think I'm getting it," I said.

"Good," Santiago said. "When do we, ah, cause this diversion?"

"Soon. How much time you need to put your men in the field?"

Santiago smiled gently and looked at the gray-haired man with glasses.

"Five minutes," he said.

"I'll give you more notice than that," I said. "Just remember, everything goes right and you get San Juan Hill to keep."

"Everything will go right," Santiago said.

"If it does, all will be hunky-dory. If it doesn't, I may get a little *pavoroso* myself."

"That might be interesting to see," Santiago said.

"No," I said. "It wouldn't be."

She sat on the floor still, leaning forward, hugging her knees. Luis stood and walked back and forth slowly, never very far from her. He was calmer now. There were no tears, though his face was still childlike.

"How did you change from Angela to Lisa?" Luis said.

"Pomona Detox," Lisa said. "Couple of Sheriff's deputies picked me up and took me there. Booze, mostly. The apple doesn't fall too far from the tree, you know? There was a social worker, used to talk to me every day, and after a while when I was sober and walking around she passed me on to a woman shrink, real upper class, had a little French accent, lived in Beverly Hills, and made a fortune listening to movie stars whine. Once a week she did pro bono work with whatever they swept up and dumped in detox. She liked me, or felt bad for me, or whatever, and she started seeing me two, three days a week. She saved my life."

"Pro bono?"

"Yeah, for free, you know? Good works."

"A woman?"

"A woman doctor," Lisa said.

"What did she do?"

"We talked," Lisa said.

"That's all?"

Lisa smiled softly.

"That's all."

"This Woody," Luis said. "Do you know where he is?"

"No."

"I will have him killed."

"He doesn't matter," Lisa said. "All of that doesn't matter now."

"What did you talk about?"

"Where I came from, where I was going, what I wanted, who I was, who I wanted to be. I didn't know much of anything about any of that."

"How could you not know who you were?"

"It's a way of talking, Luis. Certainly I didn't know who I wanted to be or what I wanted to do. The doctor said I could start by taking care of myself. I said I didn't know how. She asked me what I could do. I said I gave a hell of a blow job."

"Lisa, don't talk like that," Luis said.

"I was telling her the truth," Lisa said.

"What did she say? Did she punish you?"

"She said it was a useful skill, but not for making a living."

"A woman said that to you?"

"A woman doctor," Lisa said. *"And we talked some more and she found out about how I was a stripper DJ, and we talked about that and she got me to enroll in some radio and television school on the west side, and I got an apprentice job, Sundays only, at a 5,000-watt station in Barstow, and after a while, when I thought I could leave the shrink, I came home and changed my name and got the job at the radio station and started over."*

"You told me that Lisa was your radio name."

"I know."

"But it was your all the time new name."

"Yes."

"And no one knew your real name?"

"No."

"Not even your husband?"

"No."

"But I knew."

"Yes. I hadn't been Lisa St. Claire long enough. In my head I was still Angela. So I told you."

"Because?"

"Because I thought I loved you."

"You did love me."

"Yes," Lisa said slowly. *"Yes, I guess I did."*

Luis stopped his slow pacing. He stood beside her, looking down.

"Then why did you leave me?"

"I left the shrink too soon," she said.

Chapter 38

How is Frank?" Susan said.

"Nothing new," I said.

We were in the South End, eating dinner at Hammersley's Bistro. I was having brisket. Susan was eating chicken. The brisket was the kind of meal that Irish Catholics got posthumously if they died in a state of grace.

"I wonder," Susan said, "if his wife's situation helps keep him from recovering quicker."

"You mean so he won't have to face it? Like depressed people sleep a lot?"

"Yes. It wouldn't be conscious, of course, but if you are able to retrieve her, he may come out of it quite soon thereafter."

A guy in an expensive suit went by with a woman in an expensive suit and shot at me with his forefinger. I waved. Susan raised her eyebrows.

"Charlie O'Neill," I said. "Guy I used to know."

"Odd," she said, "he doesn't look like a thug. Is that his wife?"

"No. Business associate. Her name is Victoria Wang. I know people who aren't thugs."

"Name three."

"Charlie O'Neill, Victoria Wang, and you," I said. "Want a bite of my brisket?"

"I beg your pardon," Susan said.

The room was in one of the good-looking old brick buildings that the

South End was full of. It had a high ceiling with old beams, and an open kitchen along one side. I thought it was the best restaurant in town. On the other hand, I used to like the food in the army, so people didn't always pay attention to what I thought.

"Do you really think you can get her out?" Susan said.

"I don't think that way. I suppose I have to assume I can. But mostly I think about how I'm going to do it."

"Of course," Susan said. "The question was dumb. It's like asking a baseball player, do you really think you can get a hit? If he didn't think so, he wouldn't be doing what he does."

"You weren't really asking me that anyway," I said.

Susan smiled at me, which is always a treat.

"No, I was asking you to reassure me," she said. "Thank you for noticing."

"Hey I'm a sensitive guy," I said. "I'm scoring a shrink."

The waitress brought me a second glass of Pilsner Urquell beer, which went especially well with brisket. Susan's single glass of Merlot was sipped but slightly. A woman in an Armani suit stopped by the table and said hello to Susan.

"Sarah Gallant," Susan said. "Don't you look wonderful."

We were introduced. I agreed with Susan but thought it prudent not to say so. The two women talked for a moment. I listened. And Sarah moved on.

"I wonder how she's being treated," Susan said.

"Sarah?" I said. "She looks like she's being treated fine."

"You know I mean Lisa. Aside from the fact that she's probably a captive. We have to wonder what the conditions of her captivity are."

"Freddie Santiago says that Luis Deleon is ferocious."

"It doesn't mean he is abusing her," Susan said. "He may have what he wants."

"Which is?"

"Possession. She is under his control. It may be enough."

"It hangs over everything, doesn't it?" I said. "Even we have trouble bringing it up."

"The question of sexual abuse? Yes, it does, regardless of Lisa's past."

"Any thoughts?" I said.

"On whether he will or won't? Has or hasn't? No. Maybe the control is enough, maybe it isn't. Even if I knew them in a therapeutic relationship . . ."

"His mother was a prostitute, according to Santiago."

"Where did she turn tricks?" Susan said.

"I don't know. According to Santiago, she O.D.'d in the washroom at his club and died on the floor."

Susan paused and drank some wine.

"How old was he?"

"Deleon? Around fourteen, Santiago says."

"And no father?"

"None that anyone knows about."

"If she brought men home," Susan said, "and a lot of prostitutes do, because they have nowhere else to bring them, it would have been very difficult for him."

"I guessed that," I said.

"You are sensitive," Susan said. "They were mother and son, but they were probably a couple too. He would be very angry. And he would be very angry that she died and left him and very angry that she did it for so little reason."

"Would it lead him to sexual abuse?" I said.

"It would make him very angry," Susan said.

"And he might take it out on Lisa."

"It is easy to transfer feelings you had for one important person onto another important person."

"They both left him," I said. "He probably had sexual feelings for both. They were both whores."

I knew Susan had started with those assumptions and had already moved on. I was just showing off. Susan made one of those little head and facial motions that she made, which acknowledge that she heard you and didn't indicate what she thought of what you'd said. They probably teach it in shrink school.

"We do much better," she said, "explaining why people did things than we do at predicting what they will do."

I nodded and gave some attention to the brisket and the beer. Susan carefully cut the skin from a piece of lemon roasted chicken. She never ate any fat, being very careful of her weight, which was important, because her waist was nearly the size of my neck, and she worked out barely two hours a day.

"Would you say that you know me in a therapeutic relationship?" I said.

Susan widened her big eyes so that she looked like a Jewish Dolly Parton. She shook her head.

"I would say our relationship is more fuckative."

"Well the effect is very therapeutic," I said.

"I know," Susan said, and her wide mouth widened further into her big stunning smile. "Just doing my job."

W hat does that mean?" he said. "You left your shrink too soon?"

"I was hooking up with another bad guy—my father, Woody, all the johns I did were bad guys. Then I come back and start over, and the next thing I know I'm hooked up with you."

"I am a bad guy? I am like your father? I, who have loved you more than I love life itself?"

She shook her head.

"You love your mother, Luis. You're just working it out on me."

Luis turned from her and pressed his forehead against one of the theatrical flats.

"Do not say this," he said. "Do not tell me I don't love you."

He pounded on the flat lightly with his closed fist as he spoke. The fist keeping time with the words.

"It is to tell me that I don't exist," he said. "I am my love for you, my Angel. I have built this citadel for us, furnished these rooms for us, searched for you since you left, risked everything to bring you here. Do not tell me I do not love you."

Outside the sealed room there was thunder, but it didn't register on either of them. He turned slowly away from the painted scenery and stared at her intently.

"Do not say that I do not love you."

Still seated on the floor, hugging her knees in the dim room, she met his look and held it for a long silent moment. Then she shook her head, almost regretfully.

"Whatever you feel for me, Luis, isn't love. You think it is, but it isn't. It feels more like hate to me."

"Hate?" He seemed nearly speechless. "Hate?"

"Your old lady was a hooker. You probably hated her for it. Now you transfer that feeling onto me, you know? A woman who was with you and is now with another man?"

"You . . ." His breath came in hoarse gasps. "You . . . think . . . I am . . . like . . . that? That I am crazy?"

"It's crazy to think that you can make me love you, Luis. You can't. No one can. You can make me fear you. I do fear you. I'm afraid all the time. And you're teaching me to hate you. But I love Frank and can't stop. And I don't love you and can't start. I'd rather die than spend my life with you."

He sagged against the theatrical flat. He opened his mouth, but he didn't say anything. Then he lunged at her, dropping to his knees beside her on the floor and tearing at her clothes. She tried to push him away, but he was much too strong for her. She tried to twist away, but he grappled her back. Her blouse was torn off, he ripped at her skirt. She tried to knee him but missed, hitting his thigh. She scratched at him. He slapped her and her head jerked back. He put his left forearm under her chin and bent her back, pressing on her windpipe while he stripped her skirt from her, tearing the zipper loose with his right hand. A growling noise came from him, and the guttural sound of him gasping for breath. She grabbed his hair, trying to pull his face away from her, but she wasn't strong enough and the pressure on her throat bent her backwards as he fumbled at her last remaining clothes. She managed to turn her head and bite him on the forearm and the pressure on her throat relaxed for a moment. She twisted and rolled over and scrambled toward her bed. He came after her, grabbing at her legs, as she fumbled under the mattress for her iron pipe. She got the pipe, but he yanked her by the hair and the pipe clattered to the floor as she bent back, her legs doubled beneath her. She drove her right elbow back toward him and caught his nose and heard him grunt with pain. Then she was thrown backwards, entirely, her legs straightened beneath her and she was flat on the floor on her back. He forced himself on top of her. His long hair was tangled and wet with sweat, strands of it stuck to his face. His nose was bleeding, and the blood dripped down on her. He forced her hands back above her head and forced her thighs apart with his knees and tried to insert himself into her. She twisted her hips and struggled harder. He pressed his mouth against hers and with the force of his kiss held her head down as he tried to squirm himself into position to penetrate her. His weight pressed her against the floor, his guttural rage forced against her desperate resistance, and they lay like that on the floor in the dim light of the absurd room, locked in squirming hatred while he struggled to consummate the rape, and she twisted to prevent it. He had penetrated her often in the past, and she had liked it. But in her seemingly interminable captivity, something inside her had calcified and her resolve had achieved an opalescent density. She would resist him until he killed her. She twisted her hip and jammed her knee into his crotch. He seemed to sag, as if his strength was ebbing. Slippery with sweat and blood, she wrenched herself out from under him, scrambling after her iron bar. She got it and, lying on her side, swung it and hit him across the chest. He gasped and suddenly it was over. He slumped and his grip slackened. He fell back against the theatrical flat, his arms folded across his chest, hugging the hurt. Crouching against the far wall, naked except for her torn bra and one shoe, her face smeared with the blood from his nose, her lips swollen and bloody from his kiss, her body gleaming with perspiration, holding the bar, she snarled at him, her voice sounding like someone else's as it rasped between her teeth.

"Don't . . . you . . . fucking . . . touch . . . me," she rasped. "Don't . . . you . . . ever . . . fucking . . . touch . . . me . . . again!"

He sat empty and flaccid on the floor, defeated, leaning his back against the painted scenery where the lambs gamboled in the Arcadian meadow. His bloody face was anguished, his shirt torn, his pants open. His legs splayed out inertly before him. His shoulders began to shake. Then he put his face in his hands and his whole body began to heave, and he began once again to cry. Her gasping breath and his choking sobs made all the sound there was to be heard in the room, except for the faint sound made by the trickles of muddy water beginning to course down the walls of the room and puddle on the floor behind the theatrical flats.

Chapter 39

The sun was still somewhere out over the Atlantic, east of the city, when Chollo and I parked in front of Deleon's tenement fortress and sat silently in the car. But it could have been somewhere over the Russian steppes for all the difference it made below. The rain clouds were thick and dark and low and hid the sun entirely. We didn't talk. Everything worth saying had been said. I was clean shaven and well breakfasted, wearing a good cologne and armed to the teeth. I had a black leather sap in my right hip pocket, a Browning 9 mm automatic on my hip, and a Smith & Wesson .38 revolver in a shoulder holster. Two-gun Spenser, more deadly than an evening with Madonna.

It was a hard, steady rain that drenched down like a vengeance on the sagging slums. In the tenement complex across the street, the rain had overwhelmed the roof gutters and the dirty rain water was running down the warped clapboard sides of the buildings. I'd sat in a car and waited in a lot of slums. Most people in the crime business spent a lot of time in slums. I'd always thought that there was something Shakespearean in the conceit of crime nourished by deprivation, depravity fattening on impoverishment. The slums hadn't changed much in the years that I had been sitting in them. This one was an Hispanic slum. But that only changed the language spoken. It didn't change the slum. Slums were immutable. The ethnicities changed, but the squalor and sadness and desperation remained as constant as the movement of the stars. Finally it was probably less the poverty that bred crime

than the sour stench of racism that hung over anyplace where people are sep-
arated out by kind. Since I'd been on this case I'd smelled the smell of it and
heard the talk of it. "They have no discipline . . . they'd sell the badge for
drugs . . . spic this and Cha Cha that." I'd heard it all my life and smelled it
all my life and never liked it and never understood it. Nobody, however, had
hired me to solve the American dilemma. Right now I was supposed to get
Lisa St. Claire away from an Hispanic guy in a barrio, and, being an equal
opportunity kind of guy, I was prepared to shoot him if I had to. Probably the
easiest and most efficient approach was to hate everybody. Where have you
gone, Jackie Robinson?

I watched the rain soaking into the dry rot below, maybe stirring a few dull
roots, bringing not life but more dry rot. I thought about Lisa St. Claire and
what it must be like for her, deep inside this decaying monolith. She had no
way to know we were this close. She would know Belson would be looking
for her, but she would have no way to know if he was succeeding.

I looked at Chollo in the car beside me. He was sitting low in the seat,
his arms folded on his chest, his eyes half closed. He'd probably encountered everything Deleon had encountered, and he hadn't turned out much
better, probably. He was a bad guy, but if he told you something you could
believe him. He said he'd kill you, he'd kill you. He said he wouldn't, he
wouldn't. You could trust his word. Which was more than could be said
about a lot of people who weren't supposed to be bad guys. Besides, he was
my bad guy.

"You called him?" I said to Chollo.

"Sí."

"He knows I'm coming?"

"Sí."

"He know who Broz was?"

"Seemed to. 'Course he may figure he's supposed to know who Broz is
and he's styling."

"Doesn't matter which," I said. "Santiago's in place?"

"Sí."

I looked at my watch.

"We got half an hour," I said.

"You trust Santiago?" Chollo said.

"Absolutely not," I said. "But it's in his best interest to help us."

"And besides, we got no one else," Chollo said.

"That too," I said.

Chollo took a 9 mm Glock from under his arm and checked the load and
put it back. He took a S & W .357 revolver off his belt, made sure the cylin-
der was full, snapped it back in place, and returned it.

"I always like a revolver for backup," he said. "Not so much fire power, but you can count on it to shoot."

"That thing will shoot through a cement wall," I said.

"Sí."

We got out of the car into the hard rain. I had on a leather jacket and my Brooklyn Dodgers baseball cap. I turned the collar up on the jacket and jammed the cap down lower on my forehead. We walked across the wet street where the rain was puddling in the potholes to Deleon's door that I'd spent so much time looking at and it opened before we knocked. He was a fat guy with a grayish beard, wearing a Patriots hat, a maroon shirt, a brown leather vest, and carrying an M1 carbine. He didn't say anything as we walked past him into the gray, mildew-smelling hallway. A sagging staircase started halfway down the hall and rose along the right hand wall. The fat guy said something in Spanish and opened a door at the foot of the stairs. Chollo and I walked in, the door closed behind us, and there was Luis Deleon.

*S*he took a shower and scrubbed herself clean. When she got out, she washed her bruised face in cold water. Then she put on one of the silly robes he'd provided and walked back into her prison bedroom.

He had left without speaking to her. There had been a knock on the door and some words in Spanish. Luis had replied softly, and then remained sitting for a moment, staring at the floor between his legs, before he had dragged himself to his feet, like an old man, and adjusted his clothing. He had gone to the bathroom and washed and toweled dry. Then he'd come back, picked up her iron bar from the floor and gone out of the door without ever looking at her. He was bent slightly as if his ribs hurt. He walked as if there were no strength in him.

She gathered up the torn clothing and bundled them and put them out of sight behind one of the theater flats. The monitors were dark. They had played continuously for so long that their absence was thunderous. She sat on the bed. She felt trembly. Her breathing was still hard, and it was difficult to swallow. She was frightened at what she'd done, and determined to do it again if she had to. At the center she was unyielding, and the fact of that center made her feel stronger than she had ever felt. At the same time she was terrified at what she might have set in action.

Poor Luis! she thought. Sitting at home in front of the television, he had invented just the kind of Donna Reed mother a lonely little boy would invent. And when she left him, in his anger and his loss he had invented her replacement, Lisa St. Claire, aka Angela Richard, whore turned fairy princess. And then his replacement had, in her turn, left him for another man, and all the anger and all the frantic yearning and unreturned love and desperate need had caved in on him. He could never get us untangled. She thought of the austere French woman in Beverly Hills who had saved her life. Dr. St. Claire, whose name she had taken when she came back east and started over. You'd be proud of the way I got this one figured.

She heard the key in the lock and the door to her room opened and the quiet young Hispanic woman came in carrying some clothes. She placed them on the bed and left without a word. Lisa leaned forward slowly to look at the clothes. They were hers. The ones she'd worn when he took her. Each item laundered and ironed and neatly folded. She stared at the clean *clothes, and then looked at the dark and silent television monitors around the room. It means something, she thought, as she put on her own clothes. The feel of them, her clothes, made the hard center of her expand a little. The sound of muddy water trickling down the walls behind the stage flats was the only thing she heard.*

Chapter 40

Deleon was standing at the front window, dressed all in black, his hands clasped behind his back, staring at the rain. There was no light in the room and only the gray light of the rain-soaked day filtering in through the windows. Silhouetted against the window, Deleon looked a half a foot taller than I am, angular and strong, with big hands and thick wrists. He was wearing some kind of black vaquero outfit, with a short jacket and tight pants tucked into high boots. There were silver buttons on the cuffs of the jacket. A massive dark mahogany desk filled the far end of the room, facing the door, with a window behind it where the rain flooded down the glass in a steady shimmer. On the desk was a flat-crowned black cowboy hat. Behind the desk was a high-backed swivel chair. The floor was bare. There was some kind of brownish floral paper on the walls, which was patterned with the irregular rusty outline of water leaks past. The outside walls were sandbagged to the sill level of the windows. Along the left-hand wall, a patchy blue velvet sofa squatted unevenly. One of its ornate claw and ball legs had been replaced with a couple of bricks. On the sofa was a scrawny little geek with two braids, who had to be Ramon Gonzalez, Deleon's number-two man, the shooter. He sat sprawled out with one leg up on the sofa, in the posture of indolence. It was a state he might pretend to, but one he'd never achieved. You could tell right away that it was a pose. He'd never been relaxed in his life and he wasn't now. He had a small goatee and his eyes had the seven-mile stare that you see in some hop heads and some gunnies who really love their work. This guy appeared to be both. His left hand lay along the back of the sofa and his fingers were drumming softly on the splotchy velvet. He wore a gray hooded sweatshirt and black jeans. Around his waist was a tooled leather belt with two holsters, which were part of the belt. In the holsters were a pair of pearl-handled nines. I wouldn't know where to buy such a belt if I were ever to want one, which I would not.

Chollo nodded at the geek. The geek looked at me with his unfocused stare, as if he might jump up at any moment and begin to pull my hair. I remained calm. Deleon kept his pose, gazing out the window. I didn't care. I was here. The rest was just stalling until Santiago kicked in. And the more he posed, the less we had to stall. Ramon Gonzalez continued to stare. Chollo stood beside me, his raincoat unbuttoned, apparently indifferent to where he was and what was happening. He looked like he might nod off right there, standing upright, like a horse. Finally Deleon turned slowly from the window and looked directly at me. His face had scratches on it, and his eyes looked puffy. Along with his vaquero jacket and tight pants he had on a white silk shirt open halfway down his chest, and a bright red silk scarf knotted around his throat. He spoke to Chollo in Spanish.

"He wants to know your name, and what you are doing here."

"Speak English," I said to Deleon.

Deleon answered again in Spanish.

"He prefers to do business in his own language," Chollo said.

"So do I. And if I don't do business, no business gets done."

There was silence for a moment while Deleon digested this. Ramon Gonzalez said something and Deleon answered him.

"The geek wants to shoot you for being disrespectful," Chollo said. "But Deleon says . . ."

"You are my guest," Deleon answered. "I will accommodate your language."

"You are very kind," I said. "I am sorry that I speak only one."

"You represent Mr. Broz?" Deleon said.

He walked to his desk and leaned his hips against it and crossed his legs at the ankles and folded his arms across his chest, and looked magisterial. On the wall behind him to the right of the window, a trickle of dirty water wormed toward the floor. I wondered if Napoleon's quarters leaked.

"Yeah. We got no problem you doing distribution action up here for Mr. del Rio. Fact, you can have the whole Merrimack Valley, you can get it away from Freddie. All we want is to assure our interests."

"Which are?"

"Five percent."

"Gross or profit?"

I grinned.

"Gross," I said.

Deleon shook his head.

"That's about my margin," he said.

"Your margin is three, four hundred percent," I said. "By the time it gets sold retail it's been stepped on half a dozen times."

"Five percent of profit," Deleon said.

Another stripe of muddy water joined the first one sluicing quietly down the walls behind Deleon. The rain rattled on the windows and rolled in translucent sheets down the glass. I shook my head.

"Five percent of gross, or no deal," I said. "That's a very reasonable figure."

Deleon stood up and put his hands on his hips. He leaned forward slightly, bending at the waist, and I could see a flicker of something frightful in his eyes. He was a pretentious clown, but he was something else too. No wonder people were careful of him.

"No deal? Who the fuck are you to tell me no deal?" he said. His voice sounded as if it were forcing its way out of a very narrow passage.

"What the fuck you going to do about no deal? You think you say no deal, I do no deal? Fuck you, you Anglo asshole, and you go back and tell Joe fucking Anglo Asshole Broz that I decide what deal and what not deal, and he don't like it I'll kill him, and you and anyone else come up here."

Beside me Chollo began to applaud softly.

"*Magnifico*," he said softly. "*Magnifico*."

Deleon shifted his glance at him for a moment. He was puzzled. Was Chollo making fun of him? Deleon wasn't used to being made fun of. He decided to take it seriously.

"You unnerstand me?" he said, standing as tall as he could. The flicker in his eyes was gone. He was back to being a pretentious jerk.

"Don't be stupid," I said. "We can shut you down easy. You think Vincent del Rio is going to go against Joe Broz in Joe's own territory? Ask Chollo here, he's del Rio's guy. Ask him what happens if you don't cut a deal with Joe."

More water was running down the back wall of the office now. Deleon looked startled that I was still opposing him. He glanced at Chollo. Chollo shrugged.

"A matter of respect," Chollo said. "Mr. del Rio expect the same respect from Mr. Broz. Mr. Broz wanted to do business in LA."

Deleon was in a pickle. He wanted this deal. I could see the painful turning of wheels in his head.

Ramon Gonzalez said something to Deleon in Spanish. Deleon gave him a short answer.

"Mr. Gonzalez wants to know what's going on," Chollo said. "Mr. Deleon said shut up."

The first gunshots sounded outside and somewhere a window shattered. Gonzalez was on his feet, with both guns drawn. Deleon was standing erect, listening, trying to locate the source of the gunshots when more of them sounded. Chollo and I dropped to the floor. Something crashed through the front window and a smoke bomb went off in the room. The wet wind coming through the broken window spread the smoke rapidly. The hall door opened and someone yelled in Spanish into the room.

Chollo murmured in my ear as we lay on the floor under the pall of smoke, "Says they're being attacked by Freddie Santiago."

Deleon rushed out with Gonzalez, leaving the door open behind them. The resulting draft drove most of the smoke into the corridor and we were alone, on the floor, while outside the gunfire continued. We got carefully to our feet. I could hear the sound of bullets thudding into the house.

"Freddie's people are cutting it kind of close," I said.

"Well, it is distracting Deleon," Chollo said.

"As long as it doesn't kill us in the process," I said.

"The room where she is should be right above us," Chollo said.

The slim muddy trickle that had been leaking down from the roof garden had been joined by other trickles until finally the whole wall was sheeted with dirty water that ran steadily. She stood in the center of the room in a dry area and listened to the creak and groan of the tenement as the weight of the water-soaked earth above bore down on its brittle skeleton. She was dressed in her own clothes, and it made her feel strangely herself. Clothes make the woman, she thought. She walked to the door and tried it. The knob turned, but the padlock was in place and she couldn't get out. She shrugged. No harm trying. A piece of plaster dropped from the wet ceiling, and a short cascade of water rushed through the hole, dwindling almost at once to a steady trickle that made a continuous drip in the center of her room. This may be a good sign, she thought. His goddamned house is starting to fall apart. The lights went out. The sudden darkness was like a physical jolt. She held herself motionless for a moment, remembering where things were, tamping down the panic that came with the blackness. She took deep breaths as she stood holding herself in, smelling the wet earth smell of the room, hearing the water trickling inside and the larger rushing sound of the rain outside. The doorway, she thought. Like in earthquakes, the doorways are stronger. She moved slowly, hands ahead of her through the wet darkness toward the doorway. Found the wall, groped along it to her left, found the doorway, pressed herself against it, and waited silently for what would come. There was in her a kind of steely resignation that counterpoised her panic. She had endured all that had happened and had not broken. And something was going to happen. And she would not break. The attempted rape had been like a climax. Something would come of it. She didn't know what it would be and all she could do was wait and be ready. She heard something outside that sounded like gunshots. Was it Frank? Had he come? She twisted the door knob again knowing it was futile. She stopped and took in a deep breath and pressed herself into the shallow doorway, invisible in the drenched, reeking darkness, and said it to herself. Ready. Ready. Ready.

Chapter 41

Gunfire started popping in the house as Deleon's troops started firing back from the sandbagged window positions. There was the occasionally heavier boom of a shotgun and occasionally the rippling bursts of a light automatic weapon. Stooping low to take advantage of the sandbags, in case Santiago's gunners lost track of what they were supposed to be doing, we moved into the hallway. A man with a handgun stuck in his belt pushed past us, carrying a clear plastic bag full of shotgun shells. We moved along the interior wall, feeling the wetness where it too was soaked with muddy water.

The staircase was empty, everyone was hunkered down at a gun port by now. I wondered where the women and children were. Probably in the central yard where the bullets wouldn't reach them. As we went up, I could hear the building groaning like a ship in a storm. The walls of the stairwell were wet, and the remnant of stairwell carpet was soaking as we walked on it. Above us I heard the sound of wood twisting.

"It's the goddamned roof garden," I said to Chollo.

"The roof garden?"

"Yeah. It's been raining for three days. All the dirt on the roof. It's soaked full of water. The house is caving in under the weight."

"That makes it nice," Chollo said.

At the top of the stairs we turned left and back past the stairwell toward the front room. In the corner of the hallway, where the right wall joined the front wall, a man was crouched by the window, staying low, trying to see what was happening. He looked up at us as we came down the corridor, and frowned. We didn't look familiar. His hand went under his coat. Chollo said something in Spanish and jerked his thumb at the stairwell behind us. The guard had his gun out now, a big, stainless-steel Colt .45. He looked past us down the corridor where Chollo had pointed, and I hit him just above his right ear with the sap. He grunted and dropped the gun and staggered against the wall. I hit him again, same place, and he sighed and slid down the wall and lay still on the floor. The water running down the walls was already beginning to soak into his shirt.

"What'd you say?" I asked Chollo.

"I said, 'Luis wants you right away,'" Chollo answered.

There was a gun in his hand now, but otherwise he looked as relaxed as he had when I thought he was falling asleep in front of Deleon. I looked at the door to Lisa's room. It was padlocked. I stepped back against the far wall, feeling the wetness soak through the back of my pants where the leather jacket didn't protect it, then I lunged a kick at the door and heard the hasp screws tear in the door. I stepped back and did it again and the hasp tore loose and the door flew open. The room was completely dark. Chollo produced a small flashlight and shone it into the darkness and there was Lisa St. Claire in jeans and a tee shirt, holding an iron bar like a baseball bat, her eyes wide and startled like a deer caught in the headlights.

The gunfire sounds increased. In the wet darkness she heard someone at the door. She turned to face the door when it burst open. The light outside the door was dim, but it was too strong after the pitch darkness of her room. She squinted, trying to adjust. She could see someone in the doorway, two someones—a big man, very broad, and a slimmer man with balletic movements. Both of them had guns. Everywhere water dripped from the ceiling and slithered down the walls. He spoke. She backed into the room a little, crouching. Maybe she could get past them as they came in to get her. She spoke, without knowing what she said. Her voice sounded to her like the snarl of an animal. He spoke again. She knew him. He was Frank's friend. He'd been at the wedding with his girlfriend. She spoke without hearing herself. He spoke to her and she didn't hear him. Her world was no longer one of discourse. She felt his arm around her. She went with him, the dancer man ahead of them. The house creaked as they moved through it. The sounds of stress in the house were nearly continuous. The walls were slick with water. Holding onto the banister with her free hand, because the stairs were slippery with rain water, she went down with him. Her heart pounded. She struggled to control herself. Calm, she thought. Ready. I'm not out yet. On the stairs Luis was there. She shrank in upon herself. Words in Spanish. Then they were in the hall. Jostled. Gunshot. Out into the rain-wet, bright-black night street. Rain smell. Headlights. Silence before her. The house groaning behind her. The big man's arm still tight around her. Headlights. Her breath shallow. She felt a ripple of agoraphobic fear. She could barely breathe. Calm. Ready. She felt the rain in her face. The armed men clumped around her. The big man continued to hold his arm around her. The street seemed vast and unstructured, the figures across the street seemed remote and unreal. The buildings next door seemed distant. She felt a little dizzy, as if the earth were unstable and things might suddenly turn upside down. Luis was talking to the big man. I have to be calm, she thought. Behind her she heard the thud of something, plaster maybe, sodden with water, falling to the floor. A timber somewhere in the house gave way with a twisting screech. I have to be ready.

Chapter 42

I said, "Lisa, it's Spenser."

She said, "Get away from me." And her voice was almost a growl.

I said, "Frank sent me. I'm here to take you out."

Chollo turned the light so it shone on my face and we stood soundless for a moment while the house creaked and moaned and the gunfire popped and rippled around us.

Then she said, "Jesus God!" And I heard the pipe clatter to the floor.

Chollo turned the light back and she was walking toward me, trying to see more clearly.

"Frank's friend?" she said. "You were at the wedding. You and Susan."

"That's me," I said. "This is my friend Chollo."

"Oh my God," she said. "Oh my God. Where's Frank? Is Frank all right?"

"He's all right. We'll take you to him."

"Oh my God," she said.

And then she was in front of me and I put my arms around her and she pressed against me and began to shake.

Chollo said, "We better be moving on."

I turned her toward the door and put my left arm around her. As we moved out of the room, I took the Browning out and held it in my right hand and cocked it. A piece of plaster fell from the ceiling and I felt the floor shift beneath my feet the way the deck of a boat shifts as the boat heels on a wave. At the head of the stairs, Chollo stopped. I heard him say, "Whoops." About halfway up the stairs we were starting down was Deleon, a short automatic in his hand, and behind him Ramon Gonzalez and five or six others. Chollo screamed at them in rapid Spanish and started down the stairs. I pushed Lisa ahead of me and came down after her. Deleon paused and Chollo screamed at him again in Spanish and the men behind him turned and ran.

"The house is collapsing, we're saving Lisa," Chollo said very rapidly to me.

"Lisa," Deleon shouted.

Chollo said something urgent and Deleon turned as Chollo reached him. "Bring Lisa this way," he said. And headed down the stairs. Water was flooding down the stairwell walls now, thick with mud, rank with its passage through the decaying superstructure of the old house. The stairs began to heave a little as we went down them, and the floor in the front hallway, slippery with muddy water, was buckling beneath us. Several of Deleon's men wrenched at the front door. It was jammed by the tilt of the building. Above us I could hear rafters, floor joists snapping. Deleon reached the front door, threw the men aside and tugged on it. It still wouldn't give. The men scattered frantically. I stepped up beside Deleon and got hold of the door, my left hand over his on the knob, and we yanked it open. One of the hinges ripped loose as we did it, and the door hung crazily inward. Everyone tried to go through it at once. Deleon turned and shoved his men aside. In a panic one of them tried to squeeze by him and Deleon shot him in the forehead. Then he turned and braced his back against the surging crowd and said "Lisa," and I shoved her past him, ahead of me out the front door and into the rain. Chollo was behind me and Deleon behind him. Somewhere in the darkness car headlights came on and the street was blinding bright, glistening in the suddenly silvery rain. Behind us more of Deleon's men poured out of the building, as more timbers tore with a wrenching splinter. The left corner, where Lisa had been a few moments ago, collapsed slowly, like an elephant dying, and as it broke up it fell faster until it came down with a roar. At the naked end of the building, one piece of plywood, hanging by a single nail, swayed back and forth above the rubble where plaster dust rose thickly in the wet air.

"When you spring someone," Chollo said, "you spring someone."

The crowd of confused gunmen crowded around us, squinting into the bright headlights. The firing had stopped. Lisa stood pressed against me, and as Deleon came toward us, she pressed in hard behind me.

"Lisa," Deleon said.

She moved behind me. I turned a little, keeping myself between him and her.

"Get away from her," Deleon said.

He moved to go around me. I could feel Lisa's hands clutching at the back of my jacket. From the corner of my eye, I saw Chollo step a little away from us to improve his angle, the big automatic hanging loosely by his side. Deleon got the inhuman flicker in his eyes again. He put a hand on my left shoulder and tried to spin me out of the way. I didn't spin. He was startled. He pushed harder. Still I was in his way. He brought his right hand up with the short automatic in it.

Chollo said, "Spenser."

I slapped the gun aside with my left hand and hit him solidly on the beezer with a straight overhand right. Blood spurted from his nose, he stepped backwards and sat suddenly down on the glistening street, in the glare of the headlights. The gun fell from his hand and I kicked it out of sight toward the cars into the darkness. I had my Browning out and cocked by the time Chollo shot Ramon Gonzalez. Gonzalez spun full around, took three running steps toward the collapsing house, and fell face forward, his arms out ahead of him. His two pearl-handled pistols skittered along the wet asphalt and banged against the curb. For a moment there was no sound but the echoing silence that always comes after gunfire. The troops were confused. They didn't know what side we were on. Were we rescuing Lisa from the building or from them? Their fortress was collapsing, their chief pistolero had just been shot by a guy come to deal with the boss, and the boss had just got knocked on his keister by an Anglo who had come with the guy who was supposed to make the deal. Beyond the headlights their ritual enemy had gathered and they were exposed to his rifles with no cover. I was in front of Lisa, and Chollo, moving so lightly his feet seemed to reach down toward the ground, had moved behind us to face the crowd from that direction.

With his hands pressed against his nose and the blood running between his fingers, Deleon screamed *"No disparen. La mujer. No disparen."*

Behind me Chollo translated softly, "Don't shoot the woman."

Deleon felt around on the ground for his gun, didn't find it, and got to his feet, trying to stop the blood with his left hand.

"This is not your husband," he said to Lisa.

Lisa pressed closer against my back.

"No," she said, "a friend."

With a loud, wrenching crash another piece of the tenement collapsed in on itself, cascading mud and water down through the mounting rubble, damping the cloud of plaster dust that tried to rise.

"We're taking her out," I said. "No one wants her hurt."

"You are not from Joseph Broz," Deleon said slowly. Like his troops, it had all come to him too quickly. He was trying to sort it out.

"No."

"And Mister del Rio?"

"Mister del Rio don't give a fuck about you, Luis," Chollo said. "Excuse me, ma'am."

Deleon nodded slowly. He was now holding his left sleeve against his nose and having some luck slowing the blood. He looked at me as if he was starting to get it. Behind him I saw the women and children come out from one of the alleys beyond the next tenement. They crouched in the street, the children pressed in close to the women. Several of the men stood in front of them the way buffalo bulls circle the calves.

"It was a trick to get in."

"Yes."

"To get Lisa."

"Yes. Now we're going to walk away from here, past those cars."

"No."

"Yeah. We got her. We got you if we want to. Freddie Santiago is out there with fifty men. You got no place to take cover, no place to run. You start up and everyone dies. It'll be a bloodbath."

"You would leave me?" he said to Lisa.

"You'll have to kill me to keep me."

"And if I let you go?"

"We walk, you walk," I said.

"And Freddie Santiago?"

I raised my voice. "Señor Santiago," I said.

From the darkness beyond the headlights, Santiago's voice said, "I am here."

"The deal is we walk, they walk."

"I do not care about *los campesinos*," Santiago's voice said. "But Luis comes out with you."

"Peasants," Chollo translated quietly.

There was a murmur among *los campesinos,* the specifics of which were unclear but the general thrust of which was disapproval.

"That wasn't our deal," I said.

"You were going to take him out for me," Santiago's voice said.

"I didn't need to," I said. "The house fell in instead."

"I still want him taken out," Santiago's voice said. "You are the one who is changing the deal."

"I don't like the deal," I said.

"You are in no position to like it or not like it, Mr. Spenser," Santiago's voice said. "Either he comes with you, or we simply cut everyone down, you and the woman included."

Most of Deleon's troops had backed away from the confrontation by now and gathered in front of the women and children. Some of the children were crying. I had the Browning steady on Deleon's stomach. He looked at Lisa, then he looked at the trapped huddle of men, women, and children near the alley mouth. Fish in a barrel. Finally he turned his head back and stared at me for a minute. I stared back and we both knew what the deal was going to have to be. Deleon's gaze shifted to Lisa.

"I was going to let you go," he said.

She didn't answer.

"It is why I had your clothes brought to you."

She said nothing. He kept his eyes on her for a long time.

From the darkness Santiago's voice spoke again.

"Are you coming or not? I have waited a long time to catch Luis Deleon. I don't wish to wait any longer."

"Time," I said to Deleon.

Still looking at Lisa he called out in Spanish to the men and women now packed into the mouth of the alley. Chollo, as the troops had drifted toward the alley, had come around to face them and now stood beside me.

"He says he's going with Santiago," Chollo translated. "Says no shooting."

I nodded. Deleon straightened and adjusted his costume. The open silk shirt was dark with the blood from his nose, and some of the blood had dried on his face.

"It was not just craziness," he said to Lisa. "I always loved you."

"It doesn't matter," Lisa said.

Deleon nodded. He started to say something, then he stopped. I think his eyes began to tear. He turned quickly away.

"We could make a fight," Chollo said.

"And lose," I said.

"There are worse things," Chollo said.

"We're here to rescue Lisa," I said.

"Sure," Chollo said.

Deleon looked up at the dark sky for a moment, the rain hitting his face, then he began to walk toward the cars. We followed him at a distance of maybe thirty feet, Lisa between us, her right hand in mine, the Browning in my right. On the other side of her, I could hear Chollo's breath. His lips were barely parted and the air hushed over them. Chollo had his gun upright, the barrel laid against his right cheek. He was so concentrated in the moment that he moved like some sort of hunting animal as we walked toward the darkness beyond the headlights.

Deleon stopped again, just at the front bumper of one of the cars. The rain was pelting down, soaking pinkish into the dried blood on his shirt front. He looked back at Lisa.

"I would have let you go," he said and stepped into the darkness beyond the cars.

Behind us a kind of sigh came from the San Juan Hill people crowded into the alley as he disappeared. Then silence. Then the sharp snap of a handgun and then nothing at all.

Lisa said, "My God."

I put my left arm around Lisa and we walked in past the cars. As our eyes adjusted, we saw a crowd of armed men. Chollo had moved ahead of us now, pushing through them. On the ground, facedown with the rain beating on its back, was the corpse of Luis Deleon. Chollo glanced at it briefly and moved on to where our car was parked. Freddie Santiago stood next to the body, wearing a Burberry trench coat and a soft hat covered by one of those clear plastic rain protectors. I heard Lisa's breath catch.

"No need to look," I said to her.

"I can look."

We stopped. Lisa took a step away from me and stared down at the body. The rain had plastered her hair to her head and soaked her tee shirt. Nobody spoke.

"The poor bastard," Lisa said finally, her voice shaky, and turned away, and leaned against my left side. I put my arm around her again.

"I guess you've got Proctor," I said to Santiago.

"And you have the girl," he said. "It's been a pleasure doing business."

Chollo had gotten into the car and left the back door open. I heard him start the motor.

"Not for me," I said and walked with Lisa to the car and got in and took her home.

*D*riving south toward Boston, the car was heading straight into the rain, and it flooded against the windshield. The dancer drove. She was in back with the big man. In the car she pulled away from his arm. It was protective, but it was encircling as well and she could not stand to be contained even that much. They spoke. But nothing they said seemed to penetrate the crystalline stillness she was inside of. There was a conversation on the car phone. The heavy wet sound of traffic hummed in the background as they drove. Then the dark highway got brighter and they were inside of 128. Then the rain stopped and the windshield cleared. They rolled through the suburbs, where the lighted windows showed along the highway and people were living reasonable lives. The highway elevated and soon they were in the city back of the north station and then they were on the central artery. Soon they pulled in under the canopy of a hospital and she was out of the car and in the lobby. There were policemen there, some she remembered knowing. Elevator, people in the corridor, white dresses, white coats, a room where Frank sat up in the bed, clean shaven with his hair combed. She stopped inside the door. There were people in the room. The big man said something. The people lingered. He said something again, harder, and people left the room. The big man went with them. Alone. She walked slowly to the bed and looked down at her husband. He spoke. She spoke. She felt tears behind her eyes. She sat on the bed beside him and he put out his right arm and she slowly sank inside it and pressed her face against his chest and closed her eyes and saw nothing else. Later she would wonder if she'd hurt him, pressing so hard against his chest. But if she did, he didn't say so, and his arm around her held firm.

Chapter 43

It was a warm Saturday night in August, and Pearl was staying at my place while Susan and I were at her place having cocktails, and roasting fresh corn and two buffalo steaks over the charcoal on Susan's open air upper deck. The buffalo steaks came from a place in north central Mass called Alta Vista farm, and Susan liked them because they had less fat than chicken. We had the charcoal in the grill and were waiting for it to get that nice gray ash all over it, while the steaks were in the kitchen marinating in red wine, rosemary, and garlic. Since it was hot on the porch, we thought after the second cocktail that a shower would be nice, and then when we were showered and had our clothes off anyway, why not lie down for a bit in the air-conditioned bedroom, while we waited for the charcoal.

"I had lunch with Lisa St. Claire today," Susan said. "She spoke very warmly of you."

I was analyzing why Susan's body was so much better than other women's. This required me to look at it studiously, and at times, do some hands-on research. I knew it distracted her from what she was saying, but science must be served.

"Maybe it's because I rescued her from a homicidal maniac," I said.

"Probably has something to do with it . . . What are you doing?"

"Experimenting."

"Well, if you wish to, you may do it again."

"As necessary," I said. "How are she and Belson doing?"

"I think they are okay," Susan said. "For one thing, they are now dealing with the real people, not some fairy-tale people they've invented for each other."

Susan took in a deep breath and let it out slowly.

"And . . . they've both . . . learned," she said.

"Yes?" I said. "What have they both learned?"

Susan shifted a little on the bed beside me.

"I . . . don't . . . remember," she said.

"She learned that he couldn't entirely protect her," I said.

"Yes," Susan said.

"He learned that she was not a goddess who had deigned to marry him," I said.

"And . . . what . . . have . . . you . . . learned?"

"I believe I've learned how to get your attention," I said. My voice sounded a little hoarse to me.

"You've . . . known . . . that . . . for . . . years," Susan said.

She put her face very close to mine so that her lips brushed mine when she spoke. I cleared my throat, but my voice still seemed scratchy.

"No harm in retraining," I croaked.

"None."

Susan arched her body toward me. Her voice was very soft.

"Do . . . me . . . a . . . favor?" she said.

"Yes."

"Please . . . stop . . . talking," she whispered.

"We're so freshly showered," I wheezed. "Should we get all sweaty again?"

"Shut . . . up," she whispered.

So I did.